EAST SIDE ELEGY

David Coleman

NFB
Buffalo, New York

ISBN: 978-1-7324191-4-8

1.East Side Elegy. 2. Crime Fiction. 3. Murder Mystery. 4. Buffalo, New York.
5. Coleman.

Cover image © Sara Murello

NFB
<<<>>>
NFB Publishing/Amelia Press
119 Dorchester Road
Buffalo, New York 14213

For more information visit
Nfbpublishing.com

To Murphy

chuid eile i síocháin

Also by David Coleman

<u>Rust Belt Redemption: A Tom Donovan Mystery</u>
Two years ago Tom Donovan was a cop, working the rough and
tumble streets of Buffalo's East side. One fateful night he was
involved in the deaths of a Federal agent and an unarmed man

<u>Shadow Boxing: Tom Donovan Returns</u>
Buffalo New York Ex cop Tom Donovan is struggling with the
events of his recent past, both physically and mentally, when an
event from twenty two years ago captures his attention.

<u>Souvenir: The Third Book in the Tom Donovan Series</u>
Carolyn Krupp already has her hands full as a single mother
raising a special needs child. When her brother Mark is assaulted
and left for dead at the edge of a park she asks her neighbor, ex
cop turned PI Tom Donovan, to look into the matter as the police
seem to already have made up their minds that Mark was in the
wrong place at the wrong time and Karma caught up with him.

EAST SIDE ELEGY

One

Donovan opened his eyes. His cell phone was buzzing furiously on the nightstand. He was still getting used to waking up in the new place and it took him a moment to realize he was in his own bed. He picked up the phone and read the caller ID; it was his office. That in itself was peculiar because besides himself only his mother had a key for the downstairs office and it was her day off. After a few misses he hit the accept button and put the phone to his ear.

"Hello," he said, coughing the sleep out of his voice.

"Tom? Where are you?" It was in fact his mother. She came in for a few hours a week to help him with the books after he decided to start his own PI business.

"Upstairs," he replied. "What are you doing in the office ma?" He looked at the clock on his nightstand, it was 9:38 AM. He'd been up until the wee hours of the morning doing an armed security job for his friend Rob Barlow.

"I came in to drop off the mail. But that's not why I'm calling."

"Okay, so why are you calling?"

"There's someone here to see you," Rose answered.

Donovan thought for a moment. He'd only moved into the small office just off of Hertel Avenue on Saranac the week before and had yet to have anyone call the new phone number. The whole concept of having an office was sketchy itself. In the last few years he had been getting along fine without one, getting referrals from downtown law firms and the occasional job from Barlow. The problem was he'd come into an "inheritance" from his late grandfather Hugh and needed to launder it.

Most of his adult life Donovan had had a complicated relationship with Hugh. His grandfather had been a notorious bookmaker and union fixer, operating out of a bar in South Buffalo. Donovan himself, after a troubled adolescence, had been convinced by his maternal Uncle Sam to straighten himself out and become a police officer. When the old man finally died though he left Donovan a quarter million dollars in cash and a note. Donovan had considered giving the money away given its nefarious source, but every time he got close to doing so he backed down. He couldn't come up with a reasonable rationalization for keeping the money, but for some reason he just couldn't bring himself to give it away. On the advice of his grandfather's lawyer, Sidney Ableson, he started to come up with a way to legitimize his windfall. Maybe not all of it, but why not set aside some for a rainy day?

"What? Who?" he asked. The electrician and the plumber had come and gone after updating the buildings aged wiring and fixtures. He and his mother's new husband, Tony, had done the remodel themselves, adding a new wall to turn the small storefront into a reception area and a modest inner office.

His mother sighed into the phone, "I really think you should come down and speak to her, Tom."

There was a seriousness to his mother's tone that put him on edge. "Alright ma, I'll be right down."

He pulled on last night's jeans and a fresh polo shirt. He looked around the room. The upper flat hadn't been used as an apartment in years. It was even sparser than his old place on St. James. He missed his old apartment but after Carolyn and her son had moved out of the lower flat things hadn't been the same. The new downstairs neighbors had a dog that barked incessantly and they seemed either powerless or unwilling to stop it. He brushed his teeth quickly and went down the back stairwell.

He went through his office and into the reception area. His mother, standing behind the desk, looked at him and smiled nervously. An early September sun was streaming through the front windows and there was a small figure silhouetted against the light. As his eyes adjusted he made out the features of an older woman with dyed brown hair and a creased smoker's face. She was wearing an old denim jacket and jeans and clutching a large purse in front of her. It was hard to tell how old she was, she'd obviously lived a hard life. She could have been in her fifties but pass for late sixties.

"Hi, how can I help you?" Donovan asked.

"Are you Tom Donovan?" She asked looking at him through thick lensed glasses.

"Yes I am."

"My name is Irene Jaworski."

Donovan knew he had heard the name before but couldn't remember where. Irene shook her head and added, "You're the one who found my granddaughter."

It came back to him then. Over a year before he had been looking for a girl named Allison Baker, a witness to an assault who had ties to a matter he was looking into for his neighbor Carolyn. He found Allison, but it was too late. She had been a street kid who had resorted to turning tricks on Genesee Street and had been killed by a John and left in a garbage tote behind the Langfield Projects. It had taken a while to locate her next of kin, her grandmother Irene. The story got sadder, Allison had lived with her grandmother in Utica NY after her father was incarcerated for manslaughter and her mother was deemed an unfit parent by the State of New York. Allison had gotten in trouble in school, was expelled and then ran away to Buffalo. Donovan had followed the story in the news and from some of the cops he still came in contact with. An arrest had never been made and the case went cold. After a while the press lost interest too. He vividly remembered the night he found her. She'd been wrapped up in a dirty bed sheet and stuffed into the tote. She'd looked small and helpless while she was alive and in death the image was only exacerbated.

Donovan was at a loss for words momentarily. A wave of guilt washed over him. He vacillated between blaming himself for putting Allison in a bad situation and knowing that eventually the streets would eat her alive. He finally cleared his throat and said,

"I'm sorry for your loss…"

"Thank you," Irene replied. She started to say something else but stopped. There were tears welling up in her eyes.

Rose stepped up with a box of tissues. She shot Tom a look that he couldn't decipher and then said, "Irene, why don't you come over here and sit down?"

Rose guided Irene to one of the chairs off to the side of the reception area. She looked at Tom and said, "I'll make some coffee," and then disappeared into the back office.

Donovan sighed and walked over and sat next to Irene. She dabbed at her cheek with a balled up tissue and looked at him expectantly. "Ms. Jaworski," he started hesitantly, "I'm not sure what I can do that the police haven't already done."

Irene shook her head. "The police? They never got anywhere."

The last Donovan had heard the cops had questioned the man who had called Donovan to the projects to extort money for information on Allison's whereabouts. The man, Randall "R.J." Jones, was a member of the Langfield Boys gang and had been arrested on a weapons charge and an outstanding warrant for armed robbery. He hadn't given anything up, denying any involvement with the girl and claiming he never told Donovan anything about a man known only as "Tiny."

"I'm sure they're doing everything they can," he said.

She looked him in the eye. "I don't think so," she said.

"Mrs. Jaworski…"

"They say she overdosed, they say she was a junkie and she

shot up and her heart stopped."

Donovan just looked back at her.

"Ally was a lot of things, but she was no junkie!"

Now Donovan shook his head. When he was a cop he saw all kinds of kids fall prey to addiction, kids from the inner city to the wealthiest suburbs. The reaction of the families was almost always denial, at first anyway. Irene must have read his mind.

"I know what you're thinking," she said. "If she was an addict why did they only find two marks on her arm?"

"There are other ways to ingest drugs."

She glared at him. "You met her didn't you? The police told me you did? Did she seem like a junkie?"

Donovan thought for a moment. He'd only met Allison once when he rescued her from her abusive boyfriend. She been scared and traumatized, he really hadn't noticed anything else. She was a runaway turning tricks though. A natural assumption would be that she was using drugs to deaden the pain of it all.

"I really couldn't say," he offered.

"And the pathologist found marks on her neck," Irene continued. "They said it was from rough sex but..." her voice trailed off.

Rose came in with a coffee pot on a tray with three mugs, a bowl of sugar packets and a bottle of creamer. She caught Tom's eye with an expectant look in her own.

"Honestly Ma'am, I don't know what I can do for you."

"I know," Irene began, starting to tear up again, "You used to be a policeman."

Donovan looked back at her. "I was, but..."

"You know how it works then?"

Donovan shrugged. "How what works?"

"It was the same thing in Utica. The system let her down and then wrote her off."

Donovan closed his eyes. Part of what she said was true but then again Allison had made her own decisions. When he opened his eyes Rose was handing Irene a cup of coffee. As she stood up she looked at Donovan expectantly again. God dammit, he thought. Even though Allison had made those decisions, she didn't deserve to die the way she did. Especially with no one to answer for it.

"Okay," he said, "I can make a few calls."

"I can pay you," Irene said, opening her bag.

Rose was glaring at Tom. "Only if I find something, and then we'll talk about money," he said.

Rose poured herself a cup of coffee with a barely concealed smile on her face.

Two

Donovan considered a possible starting point for looking into Allison's death. In the five-plus years since he had turned in his badge a chasm had opened between himself and his former brothers and sisters in blue. At first, after the shooting, some came forward to express their sympathy and understanding while others shunned him due to the way the shooting had happened that night at the McKinley projects. Eventually, even his most vocal supporters seemed to withdraw and lose touch. His former partner had taken his own life and his uncle, a captain in the BPD who had encouraged him to become a cop in the first place, had recently retired and moved to North Carolina. He still had Sherry Palkowski, whom he had met while working for the same investigation firm a few years before. Sherry had herself joined the Buffalo PD but she and Tom had bonded while working together and still saw each other regularly. He made arrangements to pick her up for lunch that day.

"You're kidding, right?" she asked, climbing into the passenger seat of his car.

"What?

"This is your new ride?"

Donovan smiled. "Yep." He'd recently sold his 2004 Malibu and replaced it with a 2016 Malibu.

Sherry shook her head. "I thought you'd branch out a little more," she said. Sherry was one of the handful of people that Donovan had told about the money that Hugh had left him. While she never offered an opinion on the money, she'd never said he should give it away either.

"What was I supposed to do, go out and buy a Hummer with chrome wheels? In my line of work you have to keep a low profile. Besides, the Malibu is a quality automobile and I am, above all, loyal."

From Sherry's apartment in Allentown it was a short ride down Elmwood to Pano's Restaurant. While they were waiting for lunch to arrive Donovan broached the subject of Allison.

"From what I've heard they've hit a wall," Sherry answered. "Since RJ Jones decided to be a good soldier and not say a word, they've run out of leads."

Donovan thought for a moment. "Who's on it?" He couldn't remember who the paper had gone to for information when the story was still on the front page.

"Last I heard it was Prescott from Homicide and some guy from the gang task force."

Donovan knew Larry Prescott by reputation only. He was a long time veteran and had a reputation as a no nonsense detective with a good clearance rate. Mention of the gang task force made him take notice. He'd spent his last three years as a cop on it.

"Do you know who the task force guy is?" he asked.

Sherry squinted and thought. "Um…Foster, yeah, James Foster."

Shit, Donovan thought. He knew Foster. They'd had an unpleasant run in a few years previously when Donvan got tangled up with a drug dealer he'd crossed.

"You know him?" Sherry asked.

"Ah…yeah. Listen do you know anybody downtown who might have some insight into this?"

"Dante's been put on light duty since he wrenched his knee. They've got him doing clerical stuff downtown. Other than that, not really."

Dante Hightower was Sherry's former training officer. Donovan considered asking Sherry to reach out to him but immediately decided against it. He'd already put Sherry's career in jeopardy once asking her to look into another matter and for now he wanted to keep the circle tight.

"Don't say anything to him just yet," he said. "As a matter of fact, don't say anything to anybody.

"Are you sure?" she asked. "If you're worried about the Benzinger thing, that's ancient history."

Donovan shook his head. "Really," she went on. "I'm kind of a rising star if you want to know."

"I'm sure you are," he smiled back. "Just keep it under your hat for now. I've got something else I can try."

Donovan's next call was to Robert Stanley, Esquire, a lawyer who had helped him with the fall out he endured after the shooting. Donovan and Stanley had gone on to form a professional relationship with the lawyer using Donovan to track down witnesses and other matters for his other clients. Over the course of time Stanley's partners also had hired Donovan to do investigative work. When he'd called Stanley, he'd explained the situation with Irene Jaworski and Allison and asked Stanley if he had any advice. Stanley had thought for a moment and then said, "I'll tell you what, there are some inquiries I could make and I'm willing to do so as kind of a quid-pro-quo."

In Donovan's experience, Stanley wasn't cheap. He was good though and had a lot of connections throughout the courts and law enforcement. His curiosity was piqued. "Alright Bob, although lawyer speak usually makes me nervous, I'll bite. What's the deal?"

He heard Stanley chuckle. "I have a client who claims that he and his extended family are being harassed and the local law enforcement aren't taking it seriously."

"Is he in the city?" Donovan asked.

"That's part of the problem, he lives in Orchard Park but members of his family live in Buffalo. He's convinced though that it's the same people doing the harassing."

"Who is this guy?"

"I tell you what," Stanley replied. "If you're free this afternoon he'll be in my office at about 3:30. You could meet him then and see what you think. That is, if this isn't interfering with the other thing you're working on."

Donovan thought for a moment and said, "To tell you the truth I have no idea where to start with the other thing. So yeah, I can be there."

Donovan parked his car in a public garage and made the short trek over to the Ellicott Square building where Stanley's office was located. He was passed off from the receptionist to Stanley's secretary and then into Stanley's office. As soon as he entered, Stanley stood up, dressed in a crisp white shirt and silk tie. The man who had been seated across from Stanley also stood up. He had a dark complexion, with short dark hair just starting to gray at the temples and a neatly trimmed mustache. He was wearing an expensive looking suit and tie. Donovan was glad he had thought to wear a suit jacket and slacks, otherwise he would have felt underdressed.

"Come on in Tom," Stanley said. "I'd like you to meet Tariq Zaman. Tariq, this is Tom Donovan, my investigator."

Donovan shook Zaman's hand; he had a firm grip and a serious expression.

"Please have a seat," Stanley said pointing to the leather chair next to Zaman's. "Let me bring you up to speed." Stanley sat down and opened a manila folder and removed some photographs and slid them across his oak desk. "Mr. Zaman and his family own several local businesses, motels, convenience stores and supermarkets. As I explained on the phone some of the businesses are here in the city and a few more are in the suburbs."

Donovan looked at the top photograph. It looked like an old

office building. It looked like there had been red paint thrown on the wall and a crude swastika painted on the door. Several windows had also been broken.

Stanley went on, "The top picture is the entrance to an Islamic education center that Mr. Zaman opened near his office in Orchard Park.

Donovan glanced at Zaman who was frowning. "I take it this was reported to the Orchard Park police?" he asked.

"Of course," Zaman said with the slightest accent. "They said it was just vandals, teenagers probably."

Donovan looked at Stanley who looked back at him expressionless. "But you don't agree?" he asked looking back at Zaman. He looked at the next picture. It showed a storefront, probably somewhere in the city. There was a broken window behind a metal gate, more paint splatters and a garbage can tipped over with its contents strewn across the sidewalk.

"That is my cousin Amar's store on Fillmore Avenue. The window was shot out and the Buffalo police said the same thing." Zaman's voice was full of frustration.

In the last few decades, unrest in the Middle East had spurred a fresh wave of immigrants to America's shores. Like other refugees and immigrants before them, they had sought opportunity where they could find it, including Buffalo and the surrounding suburbs. A few at first, and then family and friends followed until they had formed their own communities within the community. And like the waves of Poles, Germans, Irish and Italians before them, there had been resentment, suspicion and even outright hostility towards the new wave of Yemenites, Iraqis, and Pakistanis who had settled in the area.

"But you think it's something else?" Donovan asked.

Zaman nodded. "There have been threats as well."

"What kind of threats?"

Stanley interjected, "Phone calls from blocked numbers to Mr. Zaman's office and the center, notes left in the mailbox and Mr. Zaman's cousin has had verbal threats made at his store."

Fillmore Avenue was on the city's East side, not the best neighborhood to run a business, especially for an outsider. Donovan looked at the rest of the photos. More shots of the vandalism at the center and the store.

"I can see you have your doubts Mr. Donovan," Zaman said, interrupting his thoughts. "After the first Gulf War, Saddam purged many people whom he thought were Western sympathizers. One of them was my brother Faud. He disappeared one day and was never seen again. We mistakenly believed that after Saddam was overthrown there would be peace, but soon the insurgents and the criminals came into prominence. After my son-in-law was killed by Al Qaeda I knew we had to leave. I have done my best to make a life here in America for my family and assimilate as much as possible. There has been bigotry and hate before. But never like this."

"What did the police say about the messages and the notes?" Donovan asked.

Zaman shook his head. "They said they would look into it, but so far, nothing has come of it." Zaman's cell phone buzzed and he fished it out of his pocket and looked at the screen. "I'm afraid my time is not my own," he said putting the phone back in his pocket. "My daughter is waiting downstairs." He stood up and straightened his jacket. He turned to face Donovan full on and said, "Mr. Donovan, I would not have asked Mr. Stanley for his assistance but I feel this is more than just some misguided youths. If there is anything you can do to assist my family it would be greatly appreciated." He extended his hand to Donovan who shook it.

"I'll confer with Mr. Stanley and get the details. I'll see if I can turn something up," Donovan replied. Zaman shook hands with Stanley and left the office.

Donovan looked at Stanley and raised his eyebrows. Stanley sat down again behind his desk and asked, "What do you think?"

Donovan sat down again also. "I don't know. Six months ago I would have agreed with the cops. But given the way things have been going lately…" he let his voice trail off.

"A lot of invective in the air," Stanley nodded.

"This guy's a client of yours?" Donovan asked.

"One of the junior partners does some real estate work for him. The subject of a private investigator came up and your name was the first one I thought of."

"Thanks, I think."

"So you'll look into it?" Stanley asked.

"If that's my part of the bargain, why not? And the other part of the deal?"

Stanley looked down at a legal pad on his desk blotter. "I had a feeling you'd be your usual agreeable self so I already have a call out to the coroner's office and a source at the BPD."

Donovan smiled. "I guess I'm an open book," he said. Where should I start with Zaman?"

Stanley picked up his own smart phone and punched in a few numbers. "I'm sending the details of the principal locations to your phone. You can start there to work your investigative magic."

Three

Donovan got his car from the garage and fought his way through the downtown traffic and construction until he turned West on Broadway. From there it was a short drive until he turned North onto Fillmore. He'd put the address for Zaman's cousin's store into his phone and immediately recognized the location. It was on Fillmore at the end of East Utica Street. He'd spent much of his ten year career as a police officer on the city's East side.

The store was only a block or two from where a young, aspiring gang banger had drawn a weapon on him. He was still on patrol at the time and he and his partner had been dispatched on a noise complaint. They had rolled up on the address and gotten out of the black and white and were walking towards the front of the house when a young man in a hoodie and baggy jeans burst through the front door of the weathered house. The kid looked panicked and confused. He looked at the two policemen in front of him and suddenly brought his arm up. He was holding a chrome .45. He hadn't raised it completely when Donovan and his partner spread themselves out and drew their weapons. The kid looked from one to the other and then looked straight at Donovan. It had seemed all so surreal at the time, Donovan remembered. The mixed emotions on the kid's face in those few seconds, anger, confusion, fear. He remembered his own fear and how grateful he had been that he responded reflexively instead of hesitating. The kid started to raise his weapon and Donovan felt his own finger tighten on the finger guard of his weapon. The kid then either lost his nerve or thought better of it because he dropped the gun and bolted for the side of the house. Donovan and his partner gave chase but the kid made it over a fence. He was picked up on the next block when another unit spotted him and within minutes he was cornered by three other units converging on the area. Donovan and his partner barely said a word the rest of their shift. They both seemed to realize how close they came to a cop's worst nightmare.

Donovan made his way through MLK Park. The early September, end of summer weather was in full effect. It was sunny and warm but you could still feel that autumn wasn't too far off. He took a slow ride for the next few blocks. A lot had changed in the last few years, stores closed and reopened, dilapidated houses demolished and a few replaced. But much was still the same. The corner boys were out with their hard stares and attitude. Juxtaposed against them, the school buses were dropping off a new generation of kids that there still might be hope for.

He drove by Amar Said's store, the Fillmore Express. He remembered it being owned by a man named Teddy when he was a cop. Teddy was a neighborhood guy and a solid citizen. He'd been robbed one too many times though and closed the store when Donovan was still on the job. It was a small building, probably constructed during Buffalo's boom years in the last century, when the neighborhood was bustling with Polish and German immigrants. The store took up the entire first floor and there was probably an apartment upstairs. Donovan went a few blocks past, did a U-turn and pulled up to the curb a half a block away from the store. He scanned the street.

The lot to the right of the store was vacant. There was a brick building across the street with four storefronts on the first floor, two of them closed and apartments on the second. The street seemed quiet. He knew that the real activity happened after dark and decided to come back then, more suitably attired.

He went home and checked the office answering machine. There was a call from his mother requesting a call back and a second message that gave him pause.

"Mr. Donovan, my name is Kathleen Sherman. I'm calling from the State Department of Taxation and Revenue. I would appreciate a call back at…" The message went on. Shit, Donovan thought. That can't be good.

He went upstairs and made himself a sandwich and booted up his laptop. He did a search on Tariq Zaman and the Islamic Education Center. He found a few press clippings and little else. He did another search on Allison Baker. The last article had appeared over six months ago.

Her name was mentioned in an article about Randall Jones's sentencing for armed robbery and obstruction of justice. After that there was nothing. It was approaching six o'clock. He put on his trainers and went out for a run. He'd recently started running again. Even though his knees protested, he found the sterile environment and the machines at the gym boring. He'd missed being outside running like he had since he had been a teenage boxing prodigy. He ran down to Delaware Park and did two laps around the circle before heading back to his apartment. After a shower he put on a pair of jeans and an old hooded sweatshirt. He considered where he was going and retrieved the Glock from the gun safe in his closet and put it in the concealed holster inside of his waistband.

The sun had almost set into Lake Erie when he got back to Fillmore Avenue. He parked the Chevy a few blocks from the Fillmore Express and got out. Despite the temperature having dropped about ten degrees, the street was much more alive now. There were people out walking and standing around engaged in conversations. A man walking a pit bull gave him the once over and went on his way. Act casual, Donovan reminded himself. He walked past a car, an old Dodge Omni. There was a girl who looked like she was passed out behind the wheel. He walked up to the Fillmore Express and went inside.

It was a typical inner city convenience store. There were the bare essentials on the shelves, canned food, cereal and toilet paper.

The counter and register were behind inch thick bulletproof glass, and that's where all the valuable merchandise was located. Cigarettes, forty ounce bottles and rolling papers. The young man with the dark complexion behind the counter looked at Donovan suspiciously. Donovan walked up to the counter.

"Amar?" he asked.

The young man stared at him for a moment and then said, "Amar is not here," in a thick accent.

"Will he be in tonight?"

The young man shook his head, "No, Amar is here during the day."

Sensing movement behind him Donovan turned his head. A young kid, about thirteen had entered the store. He took one look at Donovan and turned around and left. Donovan had made a conscious effort to look less like a cop, he wondered sometimes if it would ever work. He dug a business card out of his wallet and pushed it through the slot in the bottom of the glass.

"Amar's cousin wanted me to speak to him. Tell him to give me a call."

The young man picked up the card and looked at it frowning. He put it down and said, "I will tell him."

Donovan nodded and went out the door. As he was leaving, he took his phone out and pretended to make a call. He looked up and down the street. No one seemed to be looking in his or the store's direction. He pretended to dial another number. As he turned to walk back to his car he looked at the building across the street again. Two of the storefronts were deserted, the other two housed a discount cell phone store and a nail salon. The apartments on the second floor seemed to be deserted but for a split second he thought he saw the glint of something in one of the windows and then it was gone. As he approached his car he noticed the girl and the Omni were gone. He climbed into the Malibu and started the engine. He sat for a moment and looked back at the building across the street from the market. From the angle he was at all of the widows on the second floor were dark, including the second one from the right, where he had seen the glint. He started the car and pulled out onto Fillmore and drove past the Market and the building across from it. Box Avenue ran into Fillmore on the north side of the building. He considered turning, but then thought it might draw attention if someone had been watching him come out of the store. He drove north another block and turned onto Roeder Street.

Roeder was a narrow dead end street that terminated at the edge of a playground next to PS 59. A few of the lots at the end of the street were now vacant and Donovan pulled the Chevy up to the curb by the second to last lot, killed the lights and checked the mirrors for any movement or signs of life on the street. With all seeming quiet, he pulled his hood up, got out of the car and walked towards the playground. He stopped short when he heard voices from where he thought the basketball court was. He decided to cut through one of the vacant lots and then through somebody's yard onto Box Avenue. He kept a house between himself and the basketball court. The sound of a TV with the volume up high came from the house on his right. He walked quickly up the driveway and emerged onto Box Avenue. He crossed the street and quickly made his way back up towards Fillmore. There was a building behind the brick building where he had seen the glint. It was one story and made from the same faded red brick that the storefront/ apartment building was. A narrow alley ran between the two buildings with a wrought iron gate at its entrance. Donovan glanced over his shoulder from where he had come. Seeing no movement there or in front of him he walked up to the gate and peered down the alley. There was almost no light, only one remaining flood light on the back of the building was lit. From what he could see there were a few garbage totes and some old furniture. He put his hand on the gate and it moved.

He pushed the gate open as quietly as possible and eased past it into the alley. There were service doors for the first floor businesses and a door in the middle that probably went up to the apartments. The wall was covered with graffiti and the alley smelled like old garbage. Donovan stepped slowly down the alley, being careful not to trip over the detritus strewn across the ground. He remembered the window he was interested in would have been the third apartment down. He looked up at the window at the back of the apartment and it was pitch black. He stepped closer to the door in the middle of the building that led upstairs. It was an old wooden door that looked like it hadn't been used in years. Just as he reached his hand for the knob, it turned and the door swung inward. There was a tall thin man silhouetted by the low watt bulb in the landing behind him. The man froze when he saw Donovan.

"What the fuck…" the man started.

"Hey," Donovan said. The man took a step outside. He was wearing jeans and a dark jacket. He was in his thirties and something about him screamed that he wasn't from the neighborhood.

"What the fuck are you doing back here?" he growled.

"I was lookin' for Maurice." Donovan said.

The man stared hard at him. "There's no Maurice here," he replied.

"Are you sure? He gave me this address last night. Said he was selling his X- Box."

The man smirked. "Is that right?" He shook his head then. "What are you really doing back here?"

"Aw man, I told you…" Donovan started. The man started to reach inside his jacket, *damn it he was strapped*. Donovan thought about reaching under his sweatshirt for his Glock but the last thing he wanted to do was get into a gunfight in a filthy alley on the East side. He grazed an old steel garbage can with his leg. With one motion he picked the lid off the can with his right hand, and stepped towards the man. The guy had just about drawn his weapon when Donovan smashed the lid from the garbage can full into his face. The man staggered back, tripped over something on the ground and fell over backwards. Donovan didn't hesitate. He turned tail and sprinted out of the alley. As he passed through the gate he looked over his shoulder, no sign of the guy. He ran full speed down Box Avenue. There were three men walking his way.

"What's your hurry?" one of them said. He made a move to block Donovan's path but Donovan turned left and sprinted through a vacant lot. He heard the three men laughing behind him.

He looked back over his shoulder just as a sedan with its lights off raced past going in the direction he had been. He was getting a feeling that he may have bitten off more than he could chew. He was over a fence and through a yard and out onto Roeder. His car was fifty yards to his right. He glanced down to his left and he saw what looked like the Dodge Omni he'd seen before making a right onto Fillmore. He ran to his car and climbed in, started it, turned around and accelerated towards the corner.

He turned right onto Fillmore and then after a few blocks he hit a red light at the corner of East Ferry. He checked his rearview. There was a sedan behind him that looked like the same one he'd seen on Box. There was a driver and at least one other person in the car. "Shit," he said to himself. The light turned green and he turned left without signaling. A car coming the other way beeped its horn and then started to go through the intersection again, effectively cutting the sedan off. Donovan accelerated going as fast as he could without getting into an accident or being pulled over, although getting a ticket would definitely be better than getting shot. He thought about the man that he had just knocked in the head; had he been watching Amar's store? If he was one of the people harassing Amar and his cousin what would the purpose of doing surveillance on the store be? Donovan checked the mirror, there was a pair of headlights coming up quickly behind him. "Shit," he said again. He was sweating now. He pulled the hood down and punched the accelerator. He went through the red light at Jefferson with his eyes half closed, hoping he wouldn't get T-boned. The sedan, twenty yards behind him, went through the light too.

He glanced at the speedometer. He was doing sixty in a thirty MPH zone. He looked up just in time to see a windowless white van pull into the street in front of him. He locked the brakes up and skidded to a halt inches from the side of the van. The sedan skidded to a halt behind him and he heard the doors open. He was lifting up the sweatshirt to grab his Glock when the side door to the van slid open and a man jumped out pointing an automatic weapon at him through the windshield. "Shit!" he yelled. Just then his driver's side window shattered. Donovan threw up his arm to cover his face after the fact. A shower of glass had pelted him in the head and neck. He whipped his head around and looked out at where his window had just disintegrated. The guy he had clocked in the alley was staring at him with piercing blue eyes and pointing a gun at him. A trickle of blood ran down from his forehead and he had a wild look in his eyes.

"Federal agents!" he barked. "Put your hands where I can see them!"

Four

With the blue-eyed man and his associate still pointing their weapons at Donovan a third man hurried up to the driver's side door and roughly yanked him out of the car. He was spun around and pushed face first into the side of the car and he felt hands patting him down.

"What's this?" the third man growled when he found Donovan's 9mm.

"I have a concealed carry permit." Donovan replied. He glanced around and saw that there wasn't a city cop in sight. Had that been a coincidence? Traffic was light at that time of night and the few drivers that passed barely seemed to notice.

The man just grunted. He must have passed Donovan's weapon off because he then roughly pulled Donovan's arms behind his back and cuffed him. Donovan was pushed over to the side of the van and trundled inside where his cuffs were locked behind him to a steel bench that ran along the side. The man with the automatic weapon climbed in the back with him and the door slammed shut.

The van accelerated with Donovan barely keeping his balance on the bench.

He looked at the man with the AR-15. He was dressed in street clothes, jeans and a flannel jacket, but he still had Fed written all over him; the posture, the bearing, things that old clothes and a three day growth of beard couldn't conceal. There was a steel grate between the driver and the back of the van. Two men sitting up front, the driver in a ball cap and the blue eyed agent he'd assaulted. It was hard to tell where they were headed, Donovan couldn't make out any landmarks through the grate. He knew the guy with the AR-15 was watching him as they rode on in silence.

Eventually the van slowed. He tried to look out through the windshield. An overhead door was being opened in front of the van. It definitely didn't look like the Federal Building downtown where he'd been taken the last time he'd run afoul of the FBI. Donovan realized then that none of the men who had taken him had showed any kind of identification, a mild panic set in. The van came to a stop and the side door slid open. The blue eyed man, now sporting a butterfly bandage where Donovan had struck him, stood with his weapon down at his side while another man climbed in and undid the lock that had secured Donovan to the bench. "Let's go," the man with the keys said.

Donovan was pushed out of the van and almost lost his balance. The overhead door was closing behind them and it was then he noticed a faint smell of petroleum and chemicals. He knew he must be north of the city, probably near the South Grand Island Bridge. He looked around, they were in an old warehouse. There was a pile of empty wood pallets and the moldy smell of disuse in the air. The blue eyed man seized him by the arm and pulled him in the direction of a small office off to the side.

"Who are you guys?" Donovan asked. The blue eyed man said nothing. Donovan noticed three other men in the warehouse making a total of six. They were all dressed the same, old street clothes, like they were trying to blend in. But they had that sharp, alert look like they were on the job. They were all wearing jackets or sweatshirts, making it easy to conceal a weapon and a vest if necessary. He was pushed into the office and a seventh man was there seated behind a desk. Someone behind Donovan took off the cuffs and then he was pushed into a cheap office chair on the other side of the desk. The man stared hard at Donovan. He was in his late forties with close cropped hair and a square jaw. One of the other men placed Donovan's wallet on the desk and the man seated there picked it up and opened it.

"So…" Donovan began.

"Shut the fuck up," blue eyes hissed.

Donovan glanced up at him but said nothing. Definitely not the time for levity.

Another man, whom Donovan hadn't seen before came into the room with a sheaf of papers and handed it to the man behind the desk. He took a pair of reading glasses out of his shirt pocket and scanned the first three pages of the document silently. After a moment, he set the papers down and removed his glasses. He fixed Donovan with hard gray eyes.

"Mr. Donovan," he began, "Can you tell me what you were

doing in the alley behind 735 Fillmore Avenue tonight?"

Donovan looked at him and then glanced at the blue eyed man who was glaring down at him. He looked back at the man behind the desk and said, "You know who I am. It would be nice if I knew who I was talking to."

The man smirked and tapped the papers on his desk. "I understand that you can be uncooperative."

Donovan frowned. "Am I under arrest?"

"Not yet."

"I can explain the assault charge away as self-defense if that's where you want to start," Donovan said, jerking his thumb at the blue-eyed man. "Your boy here was drawing a weapon on me. He didn't identify himself then either, so I reacted naturally." In his periphery he saw the man tense.

"Alright," the man behind the desk said. "Steve, why don't you go ahead and identify yourself?"

A laminated ID card was shoved in Donovan's face. The blue-eyed man was Special Agent Steven Decker of the FBI. "We're not worried about the assault as much as to why you would be stalking around outside of a field operation."

Donovan looked back across the man at the desk. "I have no idea what you're talking about, agent...?"

"You can call me Captain Brown," the man replied. "What's your relation to the Fillmore Express Mart?"

"Captain? I didn't know the FBI had ranks now." Donovan replied.

"They don't," Brown said with a small smile. "I'm with the

Department of Homeland Security. Now that we have our intro-
ductions out of the way can you tell me what your relationship
with Amar Said is? And what the fuck were you doing behind 735
Fillmore?"

Shit, the DHS, Donovan thought. What had he gotten himself
into? He decided to come clean. "I was hired by Said's cousin,
Tariq Zaman to find out who's been vandalizing their properties
and threatening them," he said.

Brown put his glasses back on and started flipping through the
papers in front of him. "Oh, that's right, you're a private investigator." He said the words private investigator with a hint of sarcasm.

Donovan nodded, determined not to take the bait. "Yes I am."

Brown looked back up at him. "And you thought whoever
spray painted the front of the express mart would be running a
surveillance operation across the street?"

"I didn't know you were watching Said," Donovan said flatly. "Mr. Zaman was concerned that it wasn't just random acts of
vandalism. I found it odd that someone was moving around in an
apparently empty apartment across the street."

Brown shook his head. "That's a great story," he said. "Local
private dick helping out a family of poor, persecuted refugees."

"What's that supposed to mean?" Donovan asked. "Are you
guys looking at Said for something? Because I haven't even met
the guy."

Brown sat back in his chair and picked up the documents again
and turned a few pages. "We'll get back to Said," he said. "Let's
talk about you for a moment."

Donovan frowned. He had a bad feeling about where this conversation was headed.

"You were on the radar of the FBI's cybercrimes division a few years back. A known associate of Brian Dinkle."

"I haven't heard from Dinkle in two years." Donovan said.

"Well yeah, no wonder," Brown said wryly. "Dinkle's dead."

Donovan swallowed. "I didn't know that. Like I said, I haven't spoken to him since he went underground." Donovan had worked with Dinkle at Frederickson and Associates when he first became a PI. Brian Dinkle had been the firm's IT savant, where he had a talent for obtaining hard to get information.

"Underground," Brown chuckled, "no pun intended I'm sure. You can't do what Dinkle did without eventually pissing off the wrong people. They found his body in New Jersey with his head caved in."

Shit, Donovan thought. He'd considered Brian a friend when he didn't have very many.

"Which leads us to another matter," Brown said bringing Donovan back to the present. "Around the same time Dinkle was pulling his Houdini act an FBI informant and his cousin went missing."

Donovan could feel a bead of sweat forming on his temple. Information Dinkle had given him had lead him to the men who were responsible for his father and his sister's death. Donovan's grandfather Hugh had executed the men in a boat storage building and then had the bodies disposed of. He sat dumbstruck. He could try to deny everything but was unsure how much Brown and company knew.

"Nothing to say?" Brown looked at him expectantly. "No wonder. We know Dinkle had accessed information, restricted as it were, regarding Mr. McNally. Then Dinkle disappears, McNally disappears…" Brown raised his hands as he trailed off.

"Don't you believe in coincidence?" Donovan asked, trying to hide his anxiety.

"Not when your friends, the Brennans, are spotted near the last place McNally and his cousin were seen. And frankly not with your late grandfather in the mix."

Donovan shrugged. If that was all Brown had it was circumstantial. Still it meant that his secrets weren't as secret as he thought.

"And then there's Michael Manzella," Brown added.

"What about him?"

Brown looked at Donovan over his reading glasses. "He turns up dead a few days later?"

Donovan could feel his face getting hot. "It wasn't me."

"You had nothing to do with the man who killed your boss, Cal Frederickson, winding up beaten and shot behind a derelict house?"

Donovan shook his head. "What does any of this have to do with Amar Said?"

"Well from where I sit it looks like you have a history of taking the law into your own hands," Brown said. "McNally and Manzella are bad enough, but let's not forget the DEA and the unarmed suspect you shot a few years before."

"Fuck you," Donovan blurted out.

"There's that temper they mentioned in your psych evaluation," Brown shot back.

"That's confidential!"

"So is the FBI's server!" Brown yelled back.

The room fell silent and the two men glared at each other. After a moment Brown finally said, "The rules have changed, Donovan. With your past and now your meddling in a DHS investigation the government has the power to throw all kinds of grief your way. Not just you but everyone in your little circle of assholes; the Brennans, your lady cop friend. Hell, I read in the file that even your new stepdad is a jailbird. I'm sure there are different levels of dirt on all of them but it will be interesting to see what shakes out once we drain the swamp that you live in."

Donovan sat back, still angry but now with the fight draining out of him.

Brown stood. "Good, I have your attention," he said. "Now to tie it all up for you. You're going to work for us."

"What?"

"You're going to get close to Said and his cousin Zaman and report back to us."

Donovan shook his head. "I just met Zaman today and I don't even know Said. If they're running some kind of terrorist cell you really think they're going to let me into their inner circle?"

"I'm sure an accomplished investigator like yourself can figure something out," Brown said, pulling on a jacket. "We'll give you a night to think about it. If you decide you don't want to help yourself and your country then well . . . we'll just have to see what happens, won't we." Brown started to leave, then stopped at the door and added, "You'll be getting a call from us in the morning. Agent Decker, please take Mr. Donovan to his car."

Decker and another agent led Donovan back to the van. They climbed in the back and sat silently on the bench that ran along the side while the garage door was rolled up and the van pulled out of the warehouse. After a few minutes Donovan spoke up, "So, what is Said supposedly into?"

"That's classified," Decker replied flatly looking past Donovan towards the front of the van.

"Then how am I supposed to know what I'm looking for?" Donovan said shaking his head. "That is if I even agree to do your dirty work."

Decker stared at Donovan. "It would be in your best interest to cooperate, Donovan. Captain Brown isn't kidding about making things unpleasant for you if you don't."

"Who the hell is Brown anyway?" Donovan asked.

"Somebody you don't want to fuck with." The van fell silent again.

After a while the van slowed and then stopped. Donovan heard footsteps outside and then the side door slid open. "Out," was all Decker said. They were back on East Ferry Street. Donovan looked around. It looked like the spot that he'd been pulled over but there was something missing.

"Where's my car?" he asked turning back to face Decker.

Decker shrugged. "Towed, stolen," he said, "not my problem." He reached into his pocket and removed Donovan's cell phone and wallet. "Here, you can call a cab."

Donovan took them and asked, "And my nine?"

"We're going to hang onto that until we figure out whose side you're on."

"Right."

"Oh, and how are the concussion symptoms?" Decker asked.

Donovan looked at him curiously, "What are you talking about?"

"We don't want to take any chances," Decker said. His right hand flashed out and he landed a punch in Donovan's midsection, knocking the breath out of him and doubling him over.

"Have a good evening," Decker said climbing back into the van.

Five

By the time Donovan found a cab and made his way home it was after 1:00 AM. He called the number he still had for the BPD impound lot and found that his car indeed had been towed there and he would have to pay a seventy-five dollar fine to liberate it in the morning. He was exhausted and the adrenaline had long worn off, but he knew it would be hard to sleep with all that had happened that evening. He silently cursed Bob Stanley for getting him involved with Said and Zaman. That was useless he realized. It was doubtful Stanley knew that the cousins were involved in anything untoward.

Brown seemed to have his whole spotted history at his fingertips. The shooting, his association with Brian Dinkle and a suspicion of his involvement with the disappearance of Seamus McNally. Brown was obviously well connected and Donovan didn't doubt for a minute that he would follow through on the threat he made to make his life difficult.

He thought about Brian Dinkle. When he first met him he

thought he was just some eccentric techie that Cal Frederickson had hired to do IT work at the agency. Dinkle had gotten involved with a group called the Digital Underground and had been caught accessing government databases. It was Dinkle who had steered Donovan towards the men who had killed his sister and his father. Before he could confront them his grandfather, Hugh had executed them. Brian was good at what he did and Donovan thought he was smart enough to always cover his tracks. Obviously he was wrong. He wondered how much truth there was to Brown's account of Brian's death. Was it someone Dinkle had worked for or spied on? Sometime after four AM Donovan finally drifted off into a fitful sleep.

He woke up just after seven and quickly gave up on the thought of going back to sleep. He went into the kitchen and made a cup of coffee. He checked his email, found nothing of interest and then decided to go for a run. The morning air was clear and cool but it looked like it was going to be another warm day. Halfway around the loop at Delaware Park he felt his phone vibrating in his pocket. He fished it out and looked at the caller ID. It was a restricted number and he knew it could only be Brown or one of his minions.

"Donovan, it's Decker," the voice on the other end said after he answered.

"Yeah?" Donovan replied breathing hard.

"Captain Brown needs an answer."

Donovan's immediate impulse was to tell them to fuck themselves but he knew that wouldn't go over too well. "What does he want me to do?" he asked.

"You need to get intel on Said," Decker responded.

"How am I supposed to do that? I already told you guys, I've never met the man. If he's really involved in some terrorist shit he's not just going to start telling me all about it."

"Start with the cousin, Zaman," Decker replied flatly. "You've met him. Tell him you're working on some leads on his harassment beef. Work your way in that way."

"Are you looking at Zaman too?"

Decker exhaled. "That's classified."

"Zaman's a client, recommended by an attorney I have a working relationship with."

"Oh, now you're going to get all ethical?" Decker snorted. "Sorry Donovan, but national security trumps your bullshit PI code of conduct."

Donovan felt like spiking his phone onto the asphalt. He took a breath and then said, "I want to talk to Brown."

"No can do" Decker responded. "I drew the short straw and I'll be your contact. I'll be calling you for updates once a day. You'd better answer my calls and you better be giving us your all or Brown will bring the wrath of God down on you and yours."

Donovan was about to reply when he realized Decker had hung up.

Donovan finished his run back to the apartment feeling suddenly fatigued and developing a headache. He was just about to hop into the shower when his phone buzzed again.

"Tom, it's Bob Stanley," the pain behind Donovan's eyes sharpened. He knew he should tell Stanley about last night but paranoia crept in. He had no idea how far Homeland Security was up his ass but he decided not to have the discussion with Stanley over the phone.

"What's up Bob?"

"I happened to get a copy of Allison Baker's autopsy," Stanley said.

"That was quick."

"I have some resources."

Donovan knew better than to ask. "What do you make of it?"

Stanley exhaled over the line. "Well, I'm not a doctor or pathologist, as you know, but if this was going to trial I'd have a few questions."

"Such as?"

"Just off the top of my head, there was a lot of heroin in Allison's system. Probably enough to kill her. The thing is the medical examiner's report said they only found two puncture wounds on her arm. And they were fresh."

"Meaning she wasn't a regular user."

"That's the way I would read it. There weren't any other signs of injection anywhere else on her body."

Donovan thought for a moment and then said, "It wouldn't be the first time somebody OD'd on their first go-round."

"True. But I would question whether she administered the

drugs herself or someone else did."

"What do you mean?"

"There was bruising on her body that indicted she may have been restrained. Ligature marks on her body and bruising on her neck."

Shit, Donovan thought. Maybe Irene Jaworski was right. "Let me ask you Bob, if you were taking this to court what would you do?"

"I'd start with recommending a second autopsy. Preferably by an independent lab."

"Sounds expensive," Donovan said.

"It's not cheap."

"Let me think about this for a while."

"Fair enough," Stanley said. "Now what about your end? Did you have a chance to look into Mr. Zaman's problem?"

Donovan hesitated. "I went down and had a look around the cousin's store and the neighborhood last night. Didn't see anything out of place." He hesitated again and then realized Stanley was waiting for more. "I'm going to give Zaman a call and check out the outreach center."

"Sounds good Tom. Keep me posted."

"Will do," Donovan replied. The line went dead. "Shit," he said out loud.

He considered calling Sherry Palkowski for a ride to the impound lot, but ruled it out when he realized an explanation of how his car got there would be required. Sherry was one of the few people he couldn't lie to and for now the fewer people who knew about his predicament the better.

The cab arrived at the impound lot on Dart Street just after 8:30. Donovan made his way to the office where a bored look-ing security guard sat behind inch thick Plexiglas. He showed his ID, wrote a check for the fee and was directed to a parking space. Besides the broken window there was a two foot long scratch on the door. He opened the door and carefully brushed the shards of glass off of the seat. It was then he noticed the seat was damp and caught a distinct scent of urine.

"God dammit!" he growled. He looked around and not seeing any other attendants in the lot he went back to the office. The attending guard looked up from his paper. "Something wrong?" he asked.

"Yeah, somebody pissed in my car."

The guard raised his eyebrows. "It wasn't me," he said.

Donovan stared at him for a moment and then asked, "Have you got anything to dry the seat?"

The guard's shoulders sagged and he exhaled. He looked around his workspace and then reached into a crumpled Tim Hor-ton's bag and removed a handful of napkins.

"I mean like paper towels or something." Donovan added.

The guard frowned and sighed again and then got up and went into a back room. He slid a handful of cheap paper towels through the slot at the bottom of the window.

"Thanks," Donovan said through gritted teeth. The guard said nothing. He just went back to his paper.

Six

Donovan knew he would have to call the insurance company about the broken window but the weather was agreeable at the moment so he used the time he had driving back to his office to think. He had inadvertently landed in a jam. The worst part was he didn't have the resources to get out of it himself and he didn't know who he could ask for help. The Feds were all over him and Captain Brown seemed like the type to follow through on his threat to make things unpleasant for his circle of acquaintances. All he could do for now was to buy himself some time. His plan was to play along with Homeland Security, at least for the time being. He pulled over and put in the address for Zaman's outreach center in Orchard Park into his phone.

Thirty-some windblown minutes later he pulled into a lot off of Big Tree Road in Orchard Park. He remembered the former medical office from the pictures he had seen in Bob Stanley's office. Someone had attempted to clean the graffiti off of the stone wall but faint outlines of it were still visible. He parked next to the only other car in the lot, a late model Audi, and got out. He looked around, Orchard Park was one of Buffalo's more well-heeled suburbs. Not the kind of place you would expect to see vandals tagging buildings. Whoever did it had risked being seen by anyone driving by on Big Tree.

He walked to the front door and pulled on it; it was locked. There was a fairly new looking buzzer and intercom to the right of the door so he pushed the button and waited. He glanced around the entryway for any kind of closed circuit camera but saw none. A few moments passed and he was just about to push the button again when a female voice come over the intercom.

"Can I help you?" the voice said.

"My name is Tom Donovan; I'm here to see Mr. Zaman."

There was a buzz and a click and Donovan heard the door unlock. He pulled it open and went into what probably used to be the waiting room. Just then a woman came out of the first door on his left and jumped slightly when she saw him.

"Sorry," Donovan said. "I heard the door unlock and I came in."

She put her hand on her chest and smiled. She was obviously of Middle Eastern descent. She had long brown hair and large brown eyes. Donovan placed her in her mid-thirties, well dressed and very well put together. "It's alright," she said with the slightest trace of an accent. "I didn't hear you come in. I'm afraid my father is not here Mr. Donovan."

"Oh… he wasn't expecting me. It's just that I met with him

yesterday and…" Donovan paused. He wasn't sure how much the daughter knew or was supposed to know.

She nodded and smiled, with the beginnings of laugh lines showing in her olive skin. "You're the private investigator," she said.

"Uh, yes," he stammered, wondering why he suddenly felt awkward.

"I am Alia," she said. "Would you like a tour?"

"Sure."

She motioned for him to follow and turned around. He caught a scent of perfume, something expensive and quite pleasant.

The first few rooms they passed seemed to have been converted into small classrooms. Alia explained that some of them were being used for English as a Second Language classes and tutoring. One had been converted into a prayer room and the last room on the right had been turned into a makeshift television studio. The windows had been covered up and there was a modest collection of video and sound equipment gathered around two chairs in front of a blue background.

"My father hopes to have a show on the local public access channel. He wants to try to dispel the negative images people have of Islam."

Donovan nodded. Good luck, he thought, given the current political climate in the area and the country. "I admire his dedication," he said.

"But?" Alia asked smiling slightly.

"Oh, no buts," he replied. "I just know there are a lot of backward thinking people who distrust anyone that doesn't look like them, talk like them or pray like them."

She looked at him, thinking. She was beautiful, but there was a sadness in her eyes. Donovan recalled her father's story of her losing her husband in a terrorist attack.

"Your father mentioned that there have been threats made?" he asked.

She nodded. "Yes, we turned some of them over to the police, but my father kept copies. I'm afraid he isn't as trusting of the authorities as he should be."

Donovan nodded. He wanted to tell her he understood, given what the family had been through but thought it might ring hollow.

"I was just about to make a pot of tea," she said. "I could play the messages for you if you have time."

"No thank you on the tea," he replied. "But I would like to hear the recordings."

She turned to walk out of the room and turned to look back at him. "Coffee then? We have a Keurig machine in the office."

Back in the office after the coffee and tea were prepared, Alia sat in front of a laptop and played the voicemails that her father had mentioned. There were five in total. Four of them were the garden variety "Go back where you came from," and "You're not welcome here" variety. The fifth was a bit more cryptic. It was a woman's voice, calm, quiet, "You know what you need to do," it started. "The longer you wait the worse you are making it."

Donovan sat back and immediately thought that there might be more to the call than just plain harassment. Alia seemed to pick up on his thoughts.

"What is it?" she asked.

"I don't know," he said hesitating. He wondered how much she knew about her father, his cousin and the circles they moved in. "Did your father say anything about the last one?"

Alia thought for a moment and then said. "I don't know if he listened to all of them. He asked me to save them for the police."

"Can I get a copy of them?"

Alia nodded. "I can put them on a flash drive for you." She stood up again and brushed past him. Once again he caught the scent she was wearing.

"That would be great."

Seven

Donovan made his way back to his office. The sky had become overcast so as soon as he got into the reception area he took the phone book out of his mother's desk and started checking the Yellow pages for an auto glass place. He was just about to dial the number of a place nearby on Hertel Avenue when his mother walked in. She did not look happy.

"What is it?" he asked.

"Irene Jaworski," Rose began, she was shaking her head.

"What about her?"

"She had a heart attack this morning. A housekeeper at the motel found her on the floor of her room."

"Shit," Donovan exhaled. "Is she…"

"She's alive. They took her to Mercy Hospital about an hour ago."

Donovan closed his eyes.

"We should go," Rose's voice brought him back.

A half hour later they walked into the emergency room of Mercy Hospital in South Buffalo. After some confusion at the reception desk they were told that Irene was still in the Intensive Care unit under observation. The receptionist told them that only immediate family were allowed visits.

"I'm her half-sister," Rose spoke up. "I'm the only family she has. Oh, me and her nephew," she added indicating Tom.

Donovan shot his mother a look that fortunately the receptionist didn't see. She must have sensed that Rose wasn't going to take no for an answer. "Through those doors, room fourteen." She gestured over her shoulder to the double doors behind her.

They found room fourteen. The curtain was drawn and the room was semi-dark. Irene appeared to be asleep. She looked even smaller and more forlorn than she did in Donovan's office a few days before. Her skin was ashen and she had a breathing tube and IV unit hooked up to her. A monitor next to the bed beeped sporadically.

Rose walked up to the bed and looked down at Irene. Tom stepped up next to his mother and then Irene's eyes slowly opened and after a moment came into focus. A single tear rolled down her cheek.

Rose took a clean tissue from her purse and wiped Irene's cheek. She took her free hand and put it on top of Irene's. "You're in the best hospital in Buffalo," Rose said. "They'll take good care of you."

"Thank you for coming," Irene rasped. She blinked back another tear and tried to smile.

"Have they told you anything?" Rose asked.

Irene sighed. "They're going to move me as soon as a room is ready. They mentioned surgery but..." she hesitated. "It's not an option."

"What do you mean?" Donovan asked.

Irene looked at Donovan directly. "They say I have Restrictive Cardio- something or other. The lower chambers of my heart are rigid. Between that and the COPD a bypass is out of the question and I'm not a good candidate for a transplant."

Donovan felt like turning away but he held Irene's stare. "I don't know how long I have," she said. "I was hoping to see this thing through."

Donovan nodded and then he felt Rose's hand on his arm. Before he could stop himself he said, "I'll see what I can do."

They said their goodbyes and he and his mother walked silently back to her car in the parking ramp. Once they were in the car Rose went to turn the key but stopped. She looked at Donovan and said, "It's a good thing you're doing, Tom. The poor thing is just looking for some closure."

He wanted to tell her, that in his experience, the concept of closure was a myth. No one ever got over the violent, untimely loss of a loved one. He wondered if she believed in it herself, given the history of their own family.

"What are you going to do?" Rose asked.

Donovan exhaled and then said, "Bob Stanley thinks it would be useful if we had an independent inquest..." he hesitated.

"But?"

"It's not cheap to hire an outside examiner." Rose looked forward through the windshield. "I doubt Irene has two dimes to rub together.

Donovan closed his eyes and said. "I think I know where I can get the money."

———————————————

After he sent his mother home with a reassurance that he would work on Irene's case he called Bob Stanley's office. Stanley's secretary told Donovan that he was in a meeting and he would call him back. He dumped his phone on his desk, sat back and rubbed his temples. He realized he still had his jacket on and stood up to take it off. He patted the sides and remembered he had the flash drive that Alia had given him.

After he hung up his jacket he put the drive into the USB port in his laptop and took a pair of headphones out of the desk drawer. He opened up the media player and played the messages again. He skipped through the first four until he got to the only female caller, "You know what you need to do…" Something about the voice was familiar. Whoever it was hadn't bothered with a voice scramble or similar tactic to disguise her identity. His curiosity piqued, he looked up a contact and hit send.

"Decker," a voice answered.

"It's Donovan."

"Look at you, checking in like a good informant."

Donovan let it slide. "I've got something I think you should hear."

"What is it?"

Donovan put his phone on speaker. "It's a message left on the outreach center's phone." He unplugged the headphones and played the message. After it ended there was silence.

"You still there?" Donovan asked.

"Yeah," Decker responded.

"Any idea what it means?" Another moment of silence. "Decker?"

"You let us worry about the Intel," Decker responded sounding irritated. "You just gather it."

"It would help if I knew what you were looking for."

"Just figure out a way to get close to Said, Shamus. He's the one we need Intel on." Decker said and then ended the call.

Donovan sat back in his chair and rubbed his temples. He could feel the events of the last few days catching up on him. He leaned farther back and closed his eyes.

Eight

S herry turned her Camry right off of Delaware onto Hertel. Donovan hadn't answered his phone the last two times she had tried his number. She had made a few enquiries, against Donovan's advice, about the dead girl in the garbage tote, and now she had a sense that something was off about it. One of the people she had spoken to was an old Sergeant she knew who was spending his last few years before retirement on a desk at headquarters. He'd told her that the case was a sore spot for some of the brass and she'd be better off keeping her head down and minding her own business. Still, Allison Baker's death bothered Sherry. She'd heard the story first hand from Donovan, the pain and degradation Allison had experienced in her life capped off by a miserable end, and no one made to answer for it. Sherry knew Tom would be upset that she'd stuck her nose in it, but she felt that Allison deserved to be spoken for. She'd also heard something that might be of interest that may or may not have a bearing on the Baker case.

She made a left onto Saranac. It was after six o'clock and the cloud cover made it seem later than it was. She slowed down as she passed Donovan's building and saw his car parked near the wall in the alley. Was that someone leaning in the driver's side window? She accelerated and parked in front of a fire hydrant a few doors down.

She walked briskly to the mouth of the alley and saw the person who had been by Donovan's car walking towards the other end. It was a kid, about five foot five, with a dark hooded sweatshirt pulled up over his head. Sherry glanced over towards Donovan's car and saw the broken window. "God damn it," she said to herself.

The kid had reached the end of the alley and turned left onto North Park, headed away from Hertel. She started off in a jog in towards the kid. Her mind flashed briefly to her service weapon, unloaded and locked in her car. How much trouble could the kid cause though?

She got to the end of the alley and the kid either heard her or sensed that he was being followed because he broke into a run. Sherry followed suit, thankful she had worn her Doc Marten's. It started to drizzle just then, the sky seeming even darker.

The kid was fast, opening up a fifteen yard lead in a few strides. Sherry was thankful she had expended the effort she had at the gym and running outside. She kept pace for the first fifty yards and then finding another gear and with her longer stride, started gaining on the kid. "Stop, police," she yelled.

The kid didn't stop, if anything only ran faster. Sherry dug down and pumped her arms like her high school track coach had taught her. She felt a sting in her side but fought through it and finally got close enough to grab the kid's shoulder. "I said stop!"

The kid spun around, only it wasn't a kid after all. It was a woman, thirties, dark hair and eyes without a hint of panic. With a sudden movement she knocked Sherry's hand off her shoulder. Sherry reached out with her other hand but the woman knocked that away too. The two women eyed each other for a second and then Sherry watched the smaller woman step into a combat stance. Sherry started to do the same when the woman's left hand flashed out. She barely had time to move her head and even so it glanced off her ear. Next the woman spun and kicked at Sherry's leg. Sherry turned in time to protect her knee and took a half step back to find her balance.

The woman lunged at Sherry, this time with a palm directed towards her nose. She feinted right and caught the sleeve of the woman's sweatshirt then used her momentum to push past her and get behind her. Sherry grabbed the woman by the back of her sweatshirt and grabbed her wrist. She was trying to pull the woman's arm behind her when Sherry's left foot slipped slightly and she couldn't finish the twist. Sherry reached out with her right hand and grabbed the woman's shoulder. Instead of trying to break free the woman shifted her weight backwards towards Sherry, first driving an elbow into Sherry's ribs and then her head back into Sherry's nose.

Sherry saw stars and knew instantly that her nose was broken. She was still clinging to the woman's wrist when she sensed her spinning around and then something hit her. Sherry had been Tased during training at the police academy and remembered it well; the pain, the loss of muscle control. She knew that it would only last a few seconds. She hit the wet ground waited for her assailant to continue but nothing came. Slowly, as the feeling in her limbs came back, she struggled up to her hands and knees. The woman was gone.

———————————————————

Donovan awoke to someone pounding on the front door of the office. Christ, how long had he been out. He went to the outer office and saw Sherry standing outside. He undid the bolt and opened the door. Her nose was bloodied and her jacket and jeans were wet and muddy.

"Jesus, what happened to you?" he asked standing out of her way.

"I caught some psycho bitch breaking into your car," she said. She grabbed the box of tissues off of Rose's desk and started to work on her nose.

"What?"

"Fucking little bitch broke your window. I went after her but then she went all Jet Li on me."

Donovan just looked at Sherry with his mouth hanging open. She wadded up the tissues and pulled a couple more from the box. She turned and looked at him. "What?" she asked.

"The window was already broken," he said.

She frowned at him. "What do you mean?"

He shook his head. "It's a long story."

"Well she was looking in your car. And I identified myself, then she took off. I caught up to her and she turned into a wildcat." Sherry checked the tissues. There was still fresh blood so she wadded them up too and reached for more. "What the hell was that all about?"

Donovan looked at the floor, lost in thought.

"Tom, do you know this woman? She's not some crack whore looking to boost a car radio. She knows how to fight and she carries a Taser." Sherry pulled down the collar of her leather jacket, exposing the two red marks where the Taser had made contact.

"What?" he looked up at her and then paused. He thought about the woman in the Dodge Omni outside Said's store. Sherry's description of her adversary and the Taser. But why her and why now?

"I might know her," he said. He was thinking of Katrina Bedford, with whom he'd crossed paths while he was still employed by the late Cal Fredrickson. Katrina had emerged out of nowhere to help her friend Donna Shields out from under her scumbag husband and his dirty friends a few years previously and then disappeared just as quickly. In the short time Donovan had known her she had kicked his ass once and then he witnessed her kill a man who was threatening Donna with a perfect headshot from about fifty yards. But what the hell was she doing in Buffalo, showing up at a place that was being staked out by the Feds and now outside his office?

He looked up and saw Sherry looking at him expectantly. "Come on upstairs," he sighed. "I've got an ice pack and some beer in the refrigerator."

————————————————

Donovan found a pair of sweatpants for Sherry to change into and deposited her into his new recliner. Once he had her situated with an ice pack and a bottle of Flying Bison he gave her an abbreviated version of his run in with the Feds the previous evening.

"Holy crap that was you?" Sherry interrupted at one point.

"What was me?"

"An alert came out last night, multiple 911 calls about a car chase on Ferry. We were waiting to be called in for backup when dispatch told us to stand down. They said it was an FBI situation and that they had it under control."

"I wondered why the cops weren't there," Donovan added. He finished his story and took a pull off of his own beer.

Sherry removed the ice pack and asked, "So where does the woman who did *this* come in?"

"I'm pretty sure I saw her down by the market last night," he answered.

"But what does she have to do with it?" Sherry asked, shaking her head. "And why is she creeping around your back alley?"

"I'm not sure."

"But you know who she is?"

"Remember the Shields thing a couple of years ago?" Donovan asked.

"Shit, Donna Shields' psycho friend?"

"Yep, Katrina Bedford."

They fell silent for a moment and then Sherry asked, "Why would she be following you now?"

"That's just it, I'm not sure she is. She was down by the Fillmore Market and she clocked me there."

"She's got something to do with this Said guy?"

"I don't know," Donovan shook his head. ""All I know is that she took off like a bat out of hell when things went sideways. That and I think she left a message at the Islamic center in Orchard Park."

"So what is she? A Fed? CIA?"

"I have no idea," Donovan replied. "She disappeared after Gary Shields died. Brian Dinkle did a little digging but she just vanished." He hesitated. "Whatever she is or whoever she works for she's dangerous. I saw her shoot a guy in the head from about fifty yards and I'm pretty sure she did Gary Shields too. Plus, she pointed a gun at me twice and both times I had the feeling that she'd use it if she had to."

"What the fuck have you got yourself into now, Donovan?" Sherry asked shaking her head.

Donovan took another pull on his beer and then sighed. "I don't know for sure but I do know we have to be careful."

Sherry was running her thumb and forefinger over the bridge of her nose and grimacing. "Fucking bitch..." she said.

"I'm serious Sher'," Donovan interrupted her. "I've got to

figure out a way to extricate myself from this situation. Until then you may want to keep your distance from me and your head down."

Sherry looked at him indignantly. She started to say something but bit it off. "I know you're trying to protect me, I get that," she said. "But this is big, Tom. And if you think I'm okay with just standing by while you get fucked over or killed or disappeared you're wrong. I'll give you some space, but I'd better be hearing from you on a regular basis or I will be back with a vengeance."

He looked at her and realized there was no point arguing. In the five years he had known Sherry they had gone from being two distrusting strangers who shared an office to best friends. "Fair enough," he said.

Sherry stood up. "I should go" she said. She picked up the bag with her wet clothes in it and started for the door, her free hand back up on the bridge of her nose. "I gotta think of some way to explain this at work."

"Chronic nose picking?"

"Hilarious," she said looking back at him. "Shit, I forgot why I was looking for you in the first place."

"What?"

"Foster, the guy from the gang task force, the one working on the Allison Baker case? You said you knew him didn't you?"

"Yeah. Why?"

"There's a rumor going around that he's been suspended."

"For what," Donovan asked.

"Insubordination, apparently he got into a beef with his commander on the gang squad.

Donovan shrugged and asked, "What does that have to do with Allison Baker?"

"That's just it," Sherry answered. "Dante said the whole gang squad is under scrutiny. Arrests have fallen off, Intel is weak and…"

"Sherry," Donovan interrupted. "I thought I told you not to stick your nose into this."

"Relax," she said smiling slightly. "It came up in conversation over lunch, just some shop gossip."

Donovan looked at her, not sure if he totally believed her. "Go on," he finally said.

"It started with the Baker case. Homicide didn't think they were getting an ample amount of cooperation from the gang squad and went on from there. The new head of the gang squad runs a pretty closed off group. He moved his base of operations from downtown to the Fillmore station and brought his own people in."

"Who is this guy?" Donovan asked.

"Lt. Ray Hunter. Ever heard of him?"

"No." Donovan wasn't surprised. He'd been off the force for over six years. A lot of people had come and gone since then.

"Anyway," Sherry interrupted his thoughts. "I thought you'd want to know."

He smiled at her. "Okay," he said. "Thanks. And I'm sorry you had to go through this tonight."

"Hey," she smiled back. "That's why I hang around with you. It's always an adventure."

Nine

Despite the nap at his desk, Donovan was still exhausted and fell into a deep sleep that night. He woke up at eight AM, made a cup of coffee and took a shower. He pulled on a pair of jeans and a pullover and made his way down the back stairs. When he entered his office he heard his mother's voice in the reception area.

"I'd be happy to help you if I knew what this was about," she said.

Curious, he walked into the reception area and saw a woman, mid-forties with dyed blond hair standing in front of his mother's desk. She had a leather bag over her left shoulder and a file folder in her left hand. They both looked at Donovan.

"Tom, this is Kathleen Sherman from the State Department of Taxation and Finance," Rose said, reading off a business card in her hand.

Donovan swallowed, he was afraid this day would come. He'd been careful, funneling his grandfather's money into the business, but there had been few instances where he'd vague with the truth.

"Mr. Donovan?" Sherman interrupted his thoughts.

"Yes," he said, forcing a smile.

"Did you receive the letter we sent to you last week?"

"Um… I don't remember." He turned to Rose. "Mom, do you remember getting something from the state?"

Rose glared at him briefly and then recovered her composure. He'd told her a little about the money that Hugh had left him but not everything. She'd asked a few times but he'd always managed to change the subject. "I put all the mail on your desk, dear." He noticed she said the word "dear" with a little venom.

Donovan looked back at Sherman. "I am so sorry, but with just opening up and already having a pretty full load, I'm afraid a few things may have fallen through the cracks."

Sherman looked back at him flatly. "I see. Well I can recap what the letter stated." She opened the file folder and took out a few sheets of paper. "All we need is documentation of the income you used to invest in the startup of your business. The items in question are listed here." She offered the sheets to Donovan.

"Of course, no problem," he said, taking the papers.

"We'd like the records by the close of business this week."

"Ooh," Donovan started.

"Mr. Donovan…"

"Well with the transition and all and moving into this office, we're still trying to get organized."

"I understand," Sherman smiled at him. "It's just a few things though and much easier for both of us than a full blown audit."

He noticed the smile fade from her face.

"Okay," he forced another smile. "We'll see what we can dig up."

"Please do," she said. She put the file folder back into her bag then turned and left.

Donovan avoided looking in his mother's direction, but he could feel her eyes on him. "Tom?"

He looked at her and tried to look earnest, he felt like he was a kid again, breaking curfew. "It's alright mom, I'll take care of it."

Her expression was hard to discern.

"Honest ma, it's okay."

An awkward silence fell over the room. After a moment Donovan turned to retreat to the back office.

"I went to see Irene last night," his mother called after him.

Donovan turned back towards Rose. "How is she?" he asked.

"She's a tough old gal, she's hanging in there, but they want to move her to hospice." Rose looked up at Tom, staring straight at him. "She doesn't have too long, Tom."

"Did she ask about Allison?" he asked.

Rose hesitated. "No, not directly. Don't worry, I didn't say anything to get her hopes up, but I did tell her you were working on it."

Donovan nodded and went back into his office. "Damn," he thought. With the state snooping around he would have to be careful about accessing the money he had stashed. That probably meant he wouldn't be footing the bill to have a body exhumed and a private autopsy performed. He'd have to call Bob Stanley and tell him not to follow up with Dr. Patel. There was another option though, and as unappealing as he found it was the only one he could think of to find out about the death of Allison Baker; he had to talk to James Foster.

Before he could sit down at his desk he heard the outer door open into the reception area and wondered if the tax lady had forgotten something.

"Francis, what a surprise," he heard his mother say.

"Hello Rose," a voice answered.

Donovan walked out into the reception area and Whitey Brennan looked at him. The smile Whitey had on his face quickly faded.

"Tommy," Whitey said, "we have to talk."

Ten

Whitey Brennan had been Hugh Donovan's employee, number two and confidante since Tom's father had been killed years before. After his grandfather died it was Whitey, and not Tom, who took over the family businesses, legitimate and otherwise. That was fine with Donovan who had never seen eye to eye with Hugh, a situation made worse when Tom became a cop. Still Tom and Whitey were close. Whitey had been his father's best friend, and he and Tom had helped each other out of several sensitive situations in the past. Tom invited Whitey back into his office. Whitey made a face and then said, "Nah, why don't we go for a ride?" He looked at Rose and added, "That is if you can spare him for a while?"

"He's all yours," Rose replied flatly.

Once outside Donovan noticed Whitey glance up and down the street as he popped the locks on his Cadillac. He climbed in the passenger seat as Whitey started the car.

"Okay," Donovan started. "What's with all the cloak and dagger shit?"

"A Fed came by the bar today Tommy," Whitey said in a low tone. "He didn't identify himself as such right away but he mentioned your name."

"Shit," Donovan exhaled.

"Indeed," Whitey continued. "Then he mentioned Hugh and I asked him what interest was it of his. He flashed his ID, Steve something or other."

"Decker?"

"Might have been," Whitey nodded. "About six foot tall with sandy brown hair. Do you know him?"

"Unfortunately."

Whitey glanced at him suspiciously. "What the fuck is going on Tommy?"

Donovan sighed and gave Whitey an abbreviated version of how he came to be involved with Captain Brown and Special Agent Decker. He left out all of the threats that Brown had made, at least for the time being.

"I see," was all that Whitey said when he finished.

"Did he say anything else?" Donovan asked.

Whitey thought for a moment and then said, "He did mention they were looking for Seamus McNally."

"Shit," Donovan said again. "Whitey, I am so sorry."

"You've got nothing to be sorry for Tommy," Whitey interjected. "McNally was your grandad and me. You weren't supposed to be there, remember?"

They rode in silence for a while until Whitey spoke up.

"There's nothing to worry about lad. McNally won't be a problem. I worked for Hugh for too long to even consider leaving any loose ends."

The way Whitey said it gave Donovan a chill. Lifetime friend or not, it was a reminder of the side of his grandfather and Whitey's world that left him cold.

"I just wanted to give you a heads up," Whitey continued. "Be careful what you say on the phone and around others."

Donovan nodded and said, "I can make this all go away if I do what they ask."

Whitey nodded back. "Be careful with that too. The Feds aren't always good at keeping promises."

———————————————————

As soon as Whitey brought him back to his office and drove off, Donovan pulled out his phone and punched in Decker's number. Decker answered on the second ring.

"Donovan, nice of you to check in." Decker opened with.

"Listen, you fuck," Donovan started. "I told you I'd work on it alright."

"And what progress have you made since the last time we spoke?"

"Look, this isn't the only thing I've got going on at the moment…"

"Donovan!" Decker interrupted. "Not my problem. Captain Brown may or may not have mentioned that time is of the essence here. So you may want to check your priorities."

Donovan held his breath, biting back a string of obscenities that he knew wouldn't help his situation. Finally he said, "I'll get you whatever I can. Just give me some room here."

"I'll do what I can," Decker replied.

"And leave the Brennan's out of it."

"That may be hard..."

"You prick," Donovan growled. "I told you I'd play ball."

"You were warned," Decker said and then the line went dead.

Donovan pocketed his phone and realized he was still standing in front of his office. He composed himself and opened the front door. Rose was gathering her things, getting ready to leave. She looked at him and he could tell she wanted to ask what Whitey's visit was all about. Fortunately she knew better than to put him on the spot. She had told him that she was more than a little relieved that he had nothing to do with Donovan's Tavern or his grandfather's business. She was always friendly towards Whitey but Donovan knew he was a reminder of her husband's untimely demise and the shadow Hugh cast over the family.

"Tony's making lasagna," she said. "He always makes too much so you're more than welcome to come for dinner.

"Thanks mom," Donovan replied, "but I've got some calls to make."

She walked up to him and kissed him on the cheek. He looked at her and could tell she was trying to hide her concern.

"See you tomorrow?" he asked.

"Absolutely."

As soon as she was gone he went back into his office and called Bob Stanley's private number. It went to voicemail. "Bob, it's Tom Donovan," he said after the tone. "Something's come up and I'm afraid we'll have to hold off on the inquest. Call me when you can."

Things were starting to feel out of control. He knew Irene Jaworski was on borrowed time but Brown and Decker were breathing down his neck. He felt bad about Irene but in the grand scheme of things, more was at stake with Said and Zaman and the Feds. A dark thought crept in regarding Irene and her quest to know the truth about her granddaughter. It was a feeling he remembered getting later on in his career as a police officer and then later reaffirmed as he moved into the PI business; the concept of closure was a fallacy.

Eleven

Donovan tried to think of his next move while he waited for Stanley to call back. He logged into the criminal record research program he had written off as a business expense and ran a few searches. Nothing came up on the cousins, Zaman and Said, but he hadn't expected to find anything for that matter, since they both had only recently immigrated to this country. He thought of, and immediately dismissed, researching the enigmatic Captain Brown. There didn't seem to be anything the people he was dealing with didn't have an eye on. He thought about Brian Dinkle. Brian had been brilliant with computers and the web, but even he got in over his head.

Over his head, that's what Donovan was thinking when his phone buzzed with Bob Stanley's number on the caller ID.

"Tom, I got your message. What's up?"

"Kind of a long story," Donovan began. Stanley was not in the circle that knew about his inheritance. He trusted Stanley, but hadn't wanted to put that kind of strain on their relationship.

"I think I've found another way forward that will take less time. And it looks like Alison's Grandmother doesn't have a lot of time."

"What do you mean?" Stanley asked.

"Her heart's giving out on her and they can't fix it. She's at Mercy Hospital and they don't give her too long."

"Alright," Stanley replied. "I'll call Dr. Patel and tell him. I think he'll be disappointed."

"What do you mean?"

He heard Stanley flipping through some papers. "Here it is. He found something in the report I faxed him."

"Which was?" Donovan prompted.

Well just from the autopsy photos I sent him, the capillaries in her eyes had burst. He said that was typical if a person drowns or is suffocated. And since there was no water present in the lungs he assumed it was suffocation."

"What about the heroin?"

"For that he would have to exhume the body to see if the drugs were administered post mortem, even shortly after death, which is his theory."

Damn it, Donovan thought. As badly as he wanted to have it done, he had to stay on course to make sure his world didn't get turned on its ear.

He realized Stanley had stopped speaking and the silence was hanging over the line.

"Well," he hesitated, "Tell Dr. Patel thank you for that, but like I said I think I have another line of inquiry to pursue."

"Mmm, you sound a little distracted."

"Just a little under the gun at the moment. I'm fine." He was about to try to end the call when he had a thought. "There is one thing you may be able to help me with…"

"What's that?" Stanley wondered.

"The Zaman thing. I'm not getting much cooperation from the cousin, Said. Is there any way you could speak to Zaman and see if he can talk to him?"

"I'll see what I can do."

—————————————

Donovan looked at the time on his computer screen, 3:22 PM. He was getting antsy. He knew Bob Stanley had better things to do than be his go between with Zaman and Said and didn't know when the lawyer would actually make the call to Zaman or if it would do any good anyway. He knew he couldn't sit still any longer. He grabbed his keys, locked his office and went to the alley to get his car. When he got to it he realized someone had broken the side view mirror off of the driver's side door and then, to add insult to injury, had simply just dumped it onto the driver's seat. He cursed under his breath and got in, tossing the mirror onto the back seat.

Thirty minutes later he was back on Big Tree Road in Orchard Park. There were a few more cars in the small lot than the last time he had been here. He took that as a good sign. Maybe he could actually speak to Zaman, tell him he was onto something but he needed more time and access to Said. It was a lie, but he was desperate.

He put his thumb on the remote to lock the car after he got out and then remembered that it was pointless for the time being. As he walked towards the building he crossed in front of a small black SUV with a man sitting in the driver's seat. It was the cashier from the Fillmore Market with whom he had spoken the other night. Donovan noticed that he was staring at him with a look of suspicion.

As he reached the front door, it swung open and a man walked out briskly, coming face to face with Donovan. He was about the same height, but had a thin wiry frame and an unfriendly scowl on his dark complected face. Donovan knew right away that it was Amar Said.

Said looked him in the eye and something about it made Donovan uneasy. Maybe he knew who Donovan was and maybe he didn't. Said brushed past him and Donovan turned to follow him but froze in his tracks when he saw that Said's cashier/driver was already out of the car staring daggers at Donovan. He turned around and went on to the front entrance.

He entered the building. He could hear voices from down the corridor. The office door, immediately on his left was closed and it looked like the light was off behind the opaque, milky glass. Donovan went down the hallway. The first door on his right was open. There were about seven people sitting at small desks listening to an older man going over a lesson in English grammar. He walked on. As soon as he passed the classroom, Zaman and Alia came out of the last room on the right. Zaman looked agitated and Alia looked concerned. They both seemed to notice Donovan at the same time. A look of surprise crossed Zaman's face. Alia smiled at him briefly, but then seemed to remember something and the smile faded quickly.

"Mr. Zaman," Donovan said. "Sorry to drop in unannounced, but I was hoping to speak to you."

"Yes, Mr. Donovan, I was going to call you."

"I think I may have…"

"We will no longer be requiring your services," Zaman interrupted.

Donovan stared back at Zaman for a moment and noticed that Zaman was having a hard time maintaining eye contact. "I was going to tell you that I may have a lead on one of the people who left a message on your phone," he said. He looked past Zaman at Alia. Her mouth had tightened and she was looking at her father with what? Concern, distress?

Zaman turned to Alia and said something quietly, but sharply in Arabic. She looked down at the floor angrily and then walked past them towards the office. He turned back to Donovan. "The police have apprehended a local teenager who they believe is the one who vandalized this building" he said, regaining his composure, "and my cousin Amar is convinced his problem stems from a neighborhood dispute he has been dealing with."

Donovan considered asking Zaman for details but he knew it was pointless. It seemed that Said's visit had put the fear of God into Zaman and for now, at least, he was being shut out.

"Thank you for taking this on," Zaman continued. "We will

of course, compensate you for your time. Will you be billing us or shall we expect an invoice from Mr. Stanley?"

"Oh," Donovan said. "I barely did anything and I owe Mr. Stanley a favor or two. I'm sure he'll consider it part of his firm's retainer." He stepped forward and offered his hand.

Zaman shook it and Donovan noticed that Zaman's hand was perspiring. "Good luck then," he added and turned to leave. As Donovan approached the entrance he glanced over his shoulder and saw that Zaman had disappeared into one of the other rooms. He took two business cards out of his wallet and turned into the office. Alia looked up from her desk, doubt and concern in her large, brown eyes. Donovan glanced around the room quickly, there were no obvious sign of a security camera but that didn't mean there wasn't one hidden somewhere. The same went for anyone listening in. Maybe it was paranoia but he didn't want to take the chance of doing something on camera that would land him or Alia in a jackpot.

"Just in case your father has any questions or needs any help in the future…," he said, grabbing a pen off the desk and scribbling something on the back of the bottom card. "I wanted to leave you my number." Alia glanced at it quickly and clutched the cards in her hand. She looked up at Donovan. It appeared she was near tears.

She forced a smile and said, "Thank you."

Twelve

A half hour later, Donovan was sitting at the Tim Horton's at the corner of Abbott Road and Southwestern Boulevard, nursing the last dregs of his coffee. He was starting to think that his gambit wasn't going to pay off when a late model Audi pulled into the lot and Alia climbed out of the driver's side. She was wearing sunglasses and walked briskly to the entrance and came in. She took off the sunglasses and scanned the coffee shop until she spotted Donovan seated at a corner table. As she walked towards him she glanced back outside nervously, as if she had expected to have been followed. She sat down across from Donovan, wearing the same worried expression she had had at the center.

"Thank you for coming," Donovan started.

"I don't have long," she said, glancing at an expensive looking watch on her wrist.

"Did you leave the card I didn't write on your desk?"

"Yes, I know why you gave me the second card," she answered

curtly.

"Alia, I have an overpowering sense that your father may be in some kind of trouble," he said quietly.

She looked at him uncertainty, without speaking

He continued, "I also think that you wouldn't be here if there hadn't been some kind of threat made."

Alia closed her eyes and shook her head. "You don't understand," she said in a near whisper.

"I might understand more than you know."

She opened her eyes and looked at him.

"I know your father's cousin isn't who he claims to be." He knew it was a gamble, because that was all he knew, or thought he knew.

"How…" she started and then cut herself off.

Donovan picked up, "I know Amar Said is under government surveillance." She looked at him incredulously. "I shouldn't be telling you this but I'm afraid you and your father may be pulled into whatever Amar is into."

With her eyes still fixed on his, a single tear rolled down her cheek. Donovan handed her a napkin and she dabbed at it. "I thought we had left all of this behind us when we left Iraq," she said barely audibly."

"All of what? Who is Amar Said?" Donovan pressed.

She made an attempt to compose herself. She straightened up and said, "I don't believe Amar Said is his real name nor is he my father's cousin. The man who is always with him, Jusef, called him by a different name once. All my father has told me is that he and

Said did business together in Iraq and Said is the one who got us out of the country after my husband was killed."

Donovan thought for a moment. "I could see why your father would feel indebted to him, but I can't help but wonder. Is there something else Said has on your father?"

"Yes, there is more. My father has never gone into detail but I know it. He was desperate to get us out of the country and he did something with Said that I know he now regrets. Something that Said is holding over his head."

They sat quietly for a moment, lost in thought. Donovan looked at Alia, it looked like she was tearing up again. "I'd like to help you if I can," he said.

"Why would you do that?" She looked at him doubtfully.

A pang of guilt hit Donovan in the stomach, his reasons were hardly altruistic. He knew that he was acting mostly in his own self-interest, his own interest and the people around him in any event. Still, his heart went out to Alia, she had lost so much and thought that leaving Iraq might put some of the pain behind her. She was beautiful, vulnerable and he found himself drawn to her. "I've been in some pretty tough spots myself," he offered. "If it wasn't for a few friends coming to my assistance, I wouldn't be here talking to you right now."

"So now we are friends?" she said somewhat bitterly. "I don't know you and you don't know me." She glared at him. "What is it that you want, Mr. Donovan?"

He put his hands up in surrender. It was time for the truth. "I'm in this too Alia," he said.

She shook her head and made a move to stand up.

"I've done things. Things that could put me and some people I care about in jail or worse."

She studied his face, trying to tell if he was being truthful. She hadn't gotten up and stormed out so he knew at least he had a chance. "If I don't get something on Said for the government things could get very bad for me really soon." He looked at her pleading. "We can help each other."

She considered this for a moment and then reached into her bag. She took out a pen and a piece of paper. "My father has told me very little about Said," she began. "But there is a man who used to work for my father in Iraq. He can tell you more." She wrote a name and number and then pushed the paper across the table to Donovan. She stood then and looked down at him with doubt and maybe a little fear in her eyes. She looked like she wanted to say something but instead turned and walked out the door, putting her sunglasses back on as she scanned the parking lot again. Donovan looked down at the paper, the name Qadry Saleem was written in neat cursive with a phone number.

He had a lead at least, a new angle to pursue, but he had to be careful. He could dial Saleem's number and ask him directly what he knew, but Saleem didn't know him from Adam and might just shut him down reflexively and just cause more problems. He could call Agent Decker give him what he knew but would that be enough to get the Feds off his back? He decided then that for now he would try to find out more about Saleem and Said and then go to Decker. It still bothered him that he had involved Alia. The potential for collateral damage had once again reared its head. But in a way Donovan knew that she was already involved whether she knew it or not.

Donovan made his way back to his office. Maybe it was because he was still thinking about Alia or it might have been the lack of a rearview mirror, but he didn't see the car trying to pass him on Parkside Avenue. He had just passed Crescent Avenue where Parkside dipped under the railroad tracks when he heard an engine gunning right next to him. Donovan realized too late that he had been drifting into the left lane and when the kid in the Dodge Challenger passing him laid on the horn Donovan jerked the wheel to the right. Before he could correct his path, he hit the curb, bounced up and then struck the concrete wall of the underpass. He heard the sickening sound of glass shattering and plastic cracking as the car came to a stop. He pried his hands off the steering wheel and looked around. The Challenger was long gone, but now traffic in both directions was slowing down to gawk at the moron who put his car into the wall. He carefully got out to assess the damage. The headlight was smashed and the fender was split and cracked. It looked like the wheel was intact but he wouldn't know for sure until he drove on it. He climbed back in, carefully waited for an opening and then pulled the car off of the curb and back onto Parkside. The steering seemed a little off, the car was pulling towards the right. "God dammit," he said out loud.

Donovan was only a few blocks from his office so he decided to try to nurse the car back home. As he turned left onto Hertel Avenue he caught the distinctive odor of burning rubber, something must have been rubbing against the right front tire. "Shit!" he said out loud. He took the last few remaining blocks as slow as he could without drawing the ire of his fellow drivers and turned right onto Saranac and then behind his building in the alley.

He got out and looked at the front of the car again. The rubber smell was worse and he heard a distinctive hissing sound. He crouched down and looked underneath and saw a pool of something, engine coolant he assumed, forming under the car. He straightened up and found himself face to face with recently suspended Detective James Foster.

Foster looked different than he remembered. He'd taken to shaving his head and looked like he had added a little bulk to his six foot, two inch frame. But Donovan recognized the look in his eyes. It was the same look that Foster had given him when Donovan had pointed a gun at him three years before.

Thirteen

"Nice ride," Foster said, glancing at the car.

"Yeah, just got it two weeks ago. Just getting it broken in."

"So I see," Foster replied. A silence hung in the air as the two men looked at each other. The only sound was a hiss coming from Donovan's car and the faint sound of traffic from Hertel.

"So," Donovan finally started, "Just in the neighborhood?"

Foster shook his head; his expression never changing. "Hardly," he said. "I heard you're looking into an ongoing BPD investigation."

"And I heard you were suspended."

Foster glared at him. "True enough, but I still have an interest in the case."

Donovan thought for a moment and said, "And you want a fellow outsider's perspective?"

The corners of Foster's mouth turned up mirthlessly. "I don't think you and I could be categorized as the same kind of outsider."

"Oh, I don't see much difference at the moment."

"You were fired for shooting a DEA agent in the face. I was suspended for looking for the truth."

Foster's words hung in the air. Donovan bristled but then convinced himself not to take the bait. "So what brings you here then, Detective?" he asked.

Foster's expression changed ever so slightly. "Apparently we're after the same thing. The truth about Allison Baker."

Donovan looked at Foster, trying to figure him out. His stomach growled and he realized he hadn't eaten since the morning. He wanted to eat and to take care of his other problem. But here was a man with direct knowledge into Allison Baker's untimely demise and it looked like he had something to say. "Come on inside," Donovan said.

Donovan led the way into the office and locked the outer door. He guided Foster into the inner office and offered him a seat

"So, how can I help you?" he asked.

Foster looked at Donovan flatly. "The Baker case…" he hesitated.

"What about it?"

"I don't know what you know about it, other than the fact that she was a witness in your vigilante case and you were the one who found her, but it stinks."

Donovan didn't know how much to give away before finding out Foster's angle. "Agreed," was all he offered.

"It's the reason I got suspended," Foster said quietly.

Donovan nodded, imploring Foster to go on.

Foster just looked at him for a moment and then continued, "Someone connected to it is being protected..." he hesitated again.

Donovan shrugged and asked, "Who? And by whom?"

Donovan could tell Foster was also struggling to figure out how much to divulge, but he knew that given their past, Foster must be desperate to seek out his help. Finally Foster continued. "You were on the gang squad, right?"

"I was, but that was a lifetime ago."

"Did you know Ray Hunter? He's a Lieutenant now but he might have been a Sergeant or something else back then?"

"Doesn't ring a bell," Donovan said after thinking for a moment.

"Anyway, "Foster continued. "I've been on the squad for about a year and then Hunter takes command. For some reason he's given a wide berth by the brass. He moves us from HQ to a quiet little office at the Fillmore station. Says it's better to be independent and all that. Makes sense for a while and then he starts bringing in his own people, sketchy, loyal mother-fuckers, each and every one of them. The rest of us start getting phased out, picking up bullshit surveillance jobs or pushing papers around our desks. I don't say anything at first, got to go along to get along and all that, but things were starting to get weird."

"What do you mean?" Donovan prompted.

"One of my CIs was compromised and took a bullet to the back of the head."

"That's not the first time that happened," Donovan replied.

Foster shook his head. "No shit," he said. "But this guy was good, extra cautious and all that."

"What else?"

"Intel on the NBH starts to dry up. It's almost like they stopped doin' business, but everybody knows that's not the case."

The NBH gang had become a major pain in the ass when Donovan was still on the gang squad. They had solidified their grasp over a large portion of the East side by offering their competition two choices, work with us or get out of the way. They were very persuasive.

"And then," Foster continued, "me, and the guys who weren't in Hunter's inner circle got frozen out."

"How does Allison Baker fit in?" Donovan asked.

"Larry Prescott, from Homicide, he and I go back to the Housing Authority days. He caught the Baker case and asked me to help him with the locals. We pulled in RJ Jones and sweat him for about eight hours. RJ isn't giving up anything so Larry and I start to look at Jones' known associates. We're about halfway through my list when Hunter tells me I'm off the case. I call Larry and he tells me that Hunter must have pulled some strings because his captain tells him that Hunter can't spare the manpower, which is bullshit because, like I said, I've been sitting on my hands for the last month. I questioned Hunter about it and things got heated. He slapped an insubordination charge on me and one of his lackeys said that I'd made threats. I get suspended pending investigation and probably wind up off the squad and back in uniform or some shit."

Donovan thought about the few facts he did know about Allison Baker's death. He decided to float a balloon, "Does the name 'Tiny' mean anything to you?" he asked.

Foster stared at him for a moment and then said, "Why do you ask?"

"The night I found Allison's body RJ mentioned his name."

Foster took his time, "Tiny is a piece of shit named Demetrius Cantrell, a known associate of RJ Jones and a former member of the Street Kings."

"Former member?"

"Last we heard," Foster replied. "Rumor has it he sold his homies out and went to work for the NBH. He is one dumb motherfucker but he's fearless and good at intimidating people."

"Do you think he had something to do with Allison's death?"

Foster frowned and said, "That is what I want to know. We were looking for him when we got pulled off the case."

"And you think he's the one being protected?"

"Either him or someone close to him."

Donovan sat back in his chair. He looked at Foster again and wondered what his angle was.

No harm in asking now. "What do you want from me James?"

"I want to hire you."

Donovan was taken aback. "Hire me?" he asked. "To do what?"

"Find out about Cantrell. Who he's hanging with. Who he's working for."

Now Donovan hesitated. He and Foster had met under adversarial conditions while Donovan was looking for Mike Manzella.

He thought Foster had considered him an angry ex-cop, overstepping his boundaries and interfering with police business. "Why me?" he finally asked.

"You know the players," Foster answered. "And after our little dustup a few years back Ernie Santiago vouched for you. He said you were a good cop and he told me about Manzella and Cal Fredrickson and how he might have done the same thing if he was in your shoes."

Ernie Santiago had been Foster's partner at the time Foster and Donovan had first met as well as one of Donovan's first training officers back in the day. Donovan knew that not all of his former Brother's and Sister's in blue had turned their back on him, but it was still good to hear that some of his reputation had survived the incident at the McKinley Projects.

"Whatever your fees are, I'll pay them," Foster added pulling a business card from his jacket pocket.

Donovan thought about asking Foster why he just couldn't let it go but he realized it was probably the same reasons he couldn't. Allison Baker had to be answered for. "Look, James," he said. "I have been hired by Allison's grandmother to look into it but I don't know what I can do if somebody above you wants it buried." He thought about Said and Zaman then. "And to tell you the truth, I'm kind of up to my ass in something else at the moment."

Foster looked at him warily. He took a pen off of Donovan's desk and wrote something on the back of the card. "Right," he said. "I know that little girl dying like that bugs you as much as it bugs me. If what Ernie said is true I know you'll do the right thing." He pushed the card across the desk. "This is my cell number. Call me if you find anything." Foster stood up.

Donovan was about to protest when he heard a loud knock on the outer door. The two men went out into the reception area and saw a woman with short blond hair and a worried expression getting ready to knock again. Donovan recognized her as the owner of the Pharmacy around the corner on Hertel. He undid the lock and opened the door. As soon as he did he heard a siren not too far away. "Hello…" he started.

"Is that your car behind the building?" she asked excitedly.

"Um, yes it is."

"It's on fire," she said.

Fourteen

A half hour later Donovan was looking at the charred front end of his new car. The acrid smell of melted plastic and burnt oil hung in the air. Foster had simply shook his head and left as the first fire truck arrived. The police had come and gone and had instructed him to have the car removed from the alley to be either repaired or scrapped. They didn't care which as long as it was gone. The patrol sergeant had seemed rather nonchalant about the situation. Donovan was suspicious though, maybe a tad paranoid he realized, but he considered the possibility that his car had been tampered with. The sergeant seemed to think the fire was related to his accident and Donovan could see the logic, but at the same time it bothered him that he might be on somebody's shit list.

He'd thought about calling the dealership and asking about the warranty, but it was after Seven PM and he doubted he'd get a live person on the line. Instead he'd called his mother and asked to speak to her husband Tony. His mother had recently remarried after living as a widow for thirty plus years. Tony Carbone was a good man and Tom was happy for his mother, but he still didn't know if being forty years of age himself, he could think of Tony as his step-father. Tony himself had done time in prison for a mistake he made as a youth but had straightened himself out and run an auto body shop until recently retiring and leaving the business to his son Matt. Tom explained his situation to Tony and forty minutes later Matt had rolled up with a flatbed to take the Malibu away. Tony pulled in the alley behind Matt in an older Lincoln Town Car.

"Wow," Matt said, looking at the Malibu. "Didn't you just get this?"

"Yep," Donovan replied.

Tony walked up next to Donovan. "I hate to say this Tom, but I think it's jinxed."

Donovan looked at Tony. Tony looked younger than his sixty five years, a little thick but not fat, receding hairline but hair neatly trimmed. "What's jinxed?" Donovan asked.

"The car," Tony answered. "Not that I'm superstitious, but some cars just roll off the assembly line under a bad sign."

That's not superstitious at all, Donovan thought. "Can you give me an estimate for the insurance?"

"Sure thing," Tony nodded. "But in the meantime, take these." He held out the keys for the Lincoln.

Donovan looked at the Town Car. It had to be at least ten years old but it seemed to be in immaculate condition. "I was going to get a rental."

Tony shrugged, "Sure, but in the meantime go ahead and use

it. It's a loaner we keep at the shop."

"That's one of the nicest loaners I've ever seen."

Matt had attached the chains to the Malibu and had started dragging it onto the back of the flat bed. "It belonged to some poor old guy who dropped dead while we had it at the shop," Tony raised his voice over the din. "His family didn't want to pay the bill, or seemed to like him at all for that matter, so they signed it over to us."

And my car is jinxed? Donovan thought.

After he watched the Chevy get hauled away, Donovan shook hands with Tony and got some takeout from Gramma Mora's. He took the food back to his office and locked himself inside. He booted up his laptop and opened the record search program he had recently purchased for the business. The program was an upgrade over the one he had used previously and had access to more detail about any given subject. He typed in Qadry Saleem, the name that Alia had given him and got five hits within seconds. Figuring the one with an Amherst, NY address was the one he wanted, he clicked on the name. Alia had supplied a current contact number, but again, Donovan didn't want to simply cold-call Saleem and possibly spook him. He wanted to check him out in person. Dropping by Saleem's home seemed like a bad idea so he thought about finding out where he worked. Saleem had become a naturalized US citizen in 2015 and his current employer was listed as the Safeguard Security Corporation. Donovan had seen Safeguard employees all over the area, uniformed security guards at banks and shopping centers, he even thought they might be the company whose guards yell at you when you are meeting someone at the arrival ramp at the Buffalo Airport. There was a picture of Saleem that looked fairly recent. He had a shaved head and piercing brown eyes that screamed either ex-military or "don't fuck with me."

He wished he still had Brian Dinkle's expertise at his disposal. Dinkle would probably be able to find out where Saleem was posted in a matter of minutes. Thinking about Brian's untimely end though made him lose his appetite and push his unfinished Burrito away. No Dinkle meant Donovan would have to get creative.

He went on Safeguard Security's website and found an 800 number for the corporate office. He doubted he'd get anywhere with that. There was a number and address for a local office. Donovan punched the number into his phone and got a recording saying that the office was closed until eight the following morning. His creativity would have to wait until the morning.

He called a car rental company that had a location nearby on Delaware avenue. After several minutes of being on hold he was told that yes, they did have a car available but no, his business credit card seemed to be frozen. "Shit," he said out loud after he hung up.

There was a loud banging on the entry door, Donovan got up and headed in that direction. Steve Decker was standing outside, glaring in through the glass door. Donovan unlocked the door and opened it.

"Here you go," Decker said, holding out Donovan's Glock.

"What's this? A peace offering?"

"Something like that. Don't make me regret it."

"Sure," Donovan replied.

"It came back clean. Well almost clean, there was that Sheriff's deputy you put in a wheelchair last year."

Donovan wasn't going to take the bait. "Ex-deputy and convicted murderer," he said.

Decker's lip curled up in a sneer and then he turned to leave. Donovan called after him, "You don't know anything about a frozen credit card, do you?"

Decker half turned. "Nope," he said. "Probably some other fucked up aspect of your life." He climbed into his SUV.

"Asshole," Donovan said under his breath.

Fifteen

Donovan found the office for Safeguard Security in a small office building in Kenmore. It was one of those small, multi-level buildings that had been put up in the late sixties or early seventies during the height of urban flight to the suburbs. Small, cramped buildings like it were needed to house all of the insurance agents, CPAs and other services. Now many of them were half empty and showing their age. Donovan had noticed only five out of the nine offices in the building looked like they had tenants, or recently departed ones. The Safeguard unit was in the basement level. It was approaching nine AM and the door was locked and it was dark behind the smoked glass panel that ran down the side of the door. Donovan tried the local number for Safeguard and for the second time it went to voicemail. The outgoing message had claimed that the office was open at 8:00 AM.

Donovan was trying to decide if he should leave and come back later or maybe just camp out in the parking lot when he heard the external door open on the floor above him. He heard a heavy set of footsteps on the stairs and a moment later a stocky red headed man appeared in the hallway. He was wearing a black uniform shirt that was straining to hold him. He was carrying a McDonald's bag with a considerable grease stain on the bottom. He noticed Donovan and slowed for a moment and then fished a set of keys out of his pocket and said, "Are you here for an interview?"

Donovan shook his head. He held up and envelope with the Stanley, Morris and Krebs letterhead and said, "I have something for one of your employees."

The redhead glanced at the envelope and frowned. "What is it?" he asked.

Donovan smiled without humor and nodded to the door of the Safeguard office. "We should probably talk inside."

The redhead sighed and unlocked the door. The outer office was cramped, messy and smelled like fast food. The redhead plopped himself down at a desk and dumped the bag on top of a file folder marked "payroll." Donovan closed the door behind them and stood waiting for the other man to get settled. Finally the redhead leaned forward in his chair and reached for the envelope. Donovan pulled it away.

"This is confidential," he said. "I'm looking for Qadry Saleem. I believe he is employed by Safeguard."

The redhead frowned and said, "I can't give out any personal information on our employees."

"I'm not looking for personal information. I just need to locate him," Donovan replied.

"You should probably talk to our area manager," the redhead said, jerking a thumb at the inner office door behind him. "He's out of town at the moment. I could try giving him a call."

Now Donovan frowned. "This is time sensitive," Donovan said waving the envelope. "I'm afraid I don't have time for you to play phone tag with your boss."

"Then I don't think I ..."

"I'll make it easy then," Donovan interrupted. "Just tell me where Saleem is posted and I'll go away and take care of my business. It will be like we never had this conversation."

The redhead sat back in his chair making the springs creak. If he was trying for nonchalance, it wasn't working. A bead of sweat ran down his temple. "What's Saleem done?" he asked.

Donovan shook his head. "I'm not at liberty to say. What I can tell you is that you don't want to be seen as interfering with an officer of the court." He stopped and let the threat hang for a moment. It was bullshit, but he was gambling that this guy wouldn't know.

The redhead logged into his computer and typed something. "Can't you just go to his apartment?" he said with a trace of resentment.

"The fewer questions asked in this case the better," Donovan replied flatly.

Redhead shook his head again and then a page flashed up on his monitor. "He's at the Broadway Market," he said. He looked up at Donovan. "He's working at the grocery store today until 5:30."

"Thanks," Donovan said. He started to leave but stopped

and looked at the redhead. "Remember, the less said the better. We don't want to have to come back here if Saleem should get spooked."

"Right," the redhead said, reaching for his McDonald's bag.

───────────

Donovan waited until the early afternoon to head down to the Broadway Market. He hoped that the guy at the Safeguard office hadn't seen through his bullshit and tipped Saleem off. He found a spot on Lombard Street right across from the Market's west entrance and parked the Lincoln.

He was back on the East Side again. As a cop he'd patrolled the same neighborhood for more than a few years. As a member of the gang squad he'd also found himself in its proximity on more than one occasion.

The market itself was a Buffalo institution. The city had donated a parcel of land in 1888 to a group of Eastern European immigrants so they could set up a place where they could meet and buy and sell the things traditional to their culture. Donovan thought about Tariq Zaman and his people and wondered if the Germans and Poles had met with resistance from the established population in their own time. Over time it had expanded and then survived the Depression, the slow collapse of the industrial sector and then white flight to the suburbs. Even after the last of the old Polish American families had moved or died out in the 80s and 90s, the market held on to its old world flavor and traditions. It was particularly busy at Easter, when even the third and fourth generations of Eastern European ancestry came in from the suburbs to get in touch with their familial roots and try to maintain traditions. The main building itself was nothing more than a large warehouse but inside it was still a bustling marketplace, filled with sights and smells from another time. There were a few concessions made to the new neighbors, a soul food restaurant and a store that sold African clothing and jewelry, but the prevailing theme still was the bakeries, fish, meat and produce markets that had been around forever. It was one of the few places in Buffalo where you could still buy honest to goodness homemade Pierogi.

The supermarket where Saleem worked was a late addition to the market. It was a discount store and one of the few chains that still did business on the city's East side. Donovan walked inside and grabbed a basket. He looked to his right and clocked Saleem immediately. It looked like Saleem had put on a little weight since he'd had the picture taken that Donovan had seen online. His hair was still shaved almost to the scalp and he was wearing the same black uniform shirt as the redheaded guy at the office. Saleem was talking to fortyish black woman wearing a store uniform. The woman didn't look happy. Saleem looked towards Donovan and Donovan looked away.

Donovan killed about ten minutes circling the store, picking up a few non-perishable things he knew he could use at the apartment. When he came back to the front of the store, he got into the express line and after the person in front of him was finished the cashier started to scan his groceries. The next lane over the cashier that Saleem had been talking to was cashing out a younger guy with his hooded sweatshirt pulled up. Out of the corner of his eye, Donovan noticed that the cashier was randomly pushing items past the scanner without them ringing up. Saleem stood slightly off to the side, looking at his phone and pretending he wasn't watching the cashier.

"Do you have any coupons?" a voice said.

Donovan turned and looked back at the woman cashing him out. "What? No, sorry…"

"It comes to $10.78, she said."

Donovan took a twenty out of his wallet and handed it over. He might have an angle on Saleem.

He killed some more time walking around the actual Broadway market. He almost impulse bought a few things before considering he probably would wind up throwing them out after they went bad. Living single for most of his life he'd long ago given up on the concept of a full refrigerator or pantry. Instead, he grabbed a cup of coffee and went out to the Lincoln to wait.

When he got to the car he realized his phone was dead. Fortunately he'd retrieved the charger from the Malibu before they'd towed it away so he plugged it in and turned it back on. He'd missed a call from Sherry while his phone was off. She hadn't left a voice message or text so he doubted it was important.

Still, he had some time to kill before the supermarket closed so he pulled up Sherry's number and hit the dial icon.

"Donovan?" she answered on the second ring.

"What's up Sher'?"

"We're about to go to roll call, but I think I've got something for you."

Donovan paused. He could tell by the urgency in Sherry's voice that she was excited or anxious about something. He assumed it was about Allison Baker. "What is it?" he asked.

"Did you talk to Foster?"

"I did, thanks for that," he said with a little more sarcasm than he intended.

If she was fazed by his tone she let it go. "I've got a line on 'Tiny'."

"Sherry…"

"Listen Tom, I know you didn't want me to get involved and I told myself that I should respect your wishes and all that bullshit but, aren't you still curious?"

Donovan felt himself frown and exhale. He was aggravated and trying to focus on what was in front of him, which was Saleem. But she was right. Every time he thought about Allison he could vividly picture her small lifeless body in the garbage tote. The image was bad enough but the fact that no one had ever been held accountable for it was worse.

"Text me the details," he said.

"Will do, and Tom, whatever you're going to do, I want in on."

"What? No way," he said. "It's a little early in your career to be going rogue."

"And you're going to stick your nose into a hornet's nest without backup?" she shot back.

He exhaled again and checked his watch.   The store would be

closing soon and he didn't have time to get into a protracted argu-
ment with Sherry, whom he realized could be just as stubborn as he
was. "Lister Sher,' I'm not going to do anything rash."

She snorted over the line. "Yeah, that would be totally out of
character for you."

"Let me finish, smart ass. I'm neck deep in the other thing at
this exact moment, but I promise I'll keep you in the loop."

She hesitated and then said, "Okay, but If you don't I will find
you and harm you."

He didn't doubt it. They said goodbye and he cut the connection.

Five PM arrived and the clouds had rolled in off the lake. It
was warm and humid for mid- September and the threat of rain
felt imminent. Donovan had positioned the Lincoln on Lombard
Street where he could see both the main entrance to the supermarket as well as the side entrance that led to the attached parking
garage. At five after, the last few patrons were shooed out of the
main entrance and he saw the store manager locking and checking the doors. That was good. It meant that all of the employees
would probably be exiting through the garage. He crouched a little
lower into the leather seat and fixed his gaze on the door that let
out into the parking garage.

Lead gray clouds had rolled in off the lake and the air grew
heavy inside the Lincoln. It had cooled off quite a bit but the hu-
midity felt like summer's dying breath. The supermarket employees
started to drift out of the store in twos and threes until finally the
manager and Saleem walked out. Saleem was talking about some-

thing and the manager appeared to be shaking his head in agree-
ment, hoping to end the conversation. Something at the far end
of the garage seemed to catch Saleem's eye and he paused and then
shared a final thought with the manager and the two men parted.
Donovan could see over the steel railing that separated the garage
from his vantage point on Lombard. _

The cashier that Saleem had been talking to earlier was standing near an older Saturn. Her arms were crossed in front of her
and she didn't look happy. Saleem approached her, his head swivel-
ing back and forth, looking for potential witnesses.

Saleem and the cashier had a conversation then, actually it was
Saleem doing most of the talking while gesturing with his hands.
The cashier's responses were mostly limited to a few words or head
shakes. Finally they paused. They both looked around the garage
and satisfied they weren't being watched, the cashier reached into
her bag and withdrew several bills and passed them to Saleem.
Without another word she got into the Saturn and drove off.

Donovan watched Saleem watch her drive off. Saleem pocketed the bills and started to walk off in the opposite direction
towards Gibson Street. Donovan slipped out of the Lincoln
and followed. He entered the garage and was twenty feet behind
Saleem when he crossed Gibson into the parking lot across from
the market's west entrance. There was one vehicle left in the lot, an
older Mercury Mariner. Saleem was headed right for it. Donovan
closed the distance and was ten feet behind when Saleem opened
the driver's side door.

"Qadry Saleem?" Donovan called out.

Saleem whirled around with the door open. His initial look of surprise was replaced by a look of confusion and then suspicion. He stared hard at Donovan with his close set brown eyes. "Who are you?" he finally said.

Donovan took another step forward and Saleem tensed immediately. Donovan held up his phone. "I know what's going on," he said.

Saleem frowned at the phone and then at Donovan. "Who are you?" he asked again.

"I know that lady and her associate are scamming the store, and I know that instead of doing the right thing and reporting it, you're shaking her down for a cut."

A brief look of panic crossed Saleem's face but then he reclaimed his composure. "You know nothing. Fuck off," he said.

"It's all right here," Donovan said, waving the phone. "The video I have plus the store's surveillance camera lands you both in a bad place."

Saleem shook his head, but Donovan noticed he was sweating. "I have done nothing wrong," he said. He made a move to get into the Mercury.

"We'll see about that," Donovan shot back. "Although, if you give me what I want I can make this all go away."

That got Saleem's attention. Still he was going to play dumb. "I don't know what you are talking about my friend."

"Amar Said," Donovan said.

Saleem looked at Donovan again through narrowed eyes. He hesitated briefly and then reached into the Merc under the driver's seat.

Donovan didn't hesitate. He knew whatever Saleem was reaching for couldn't be good. He took two steps forward and threw his shoulder into the Merc's door. Saleem had started to straighten up. Through the window Donovan saw the old school Billy club that Saleem had retrieved from under the seat in his left hand. He put pressure on the door, pinning Saleem into the side of the car. Donovan didn't anticipate Saleem being as strong as he was. With a sudden burst he pushed himself away from the car and freed himself. Donovan took a step back and regained his footing. Saleem squared himself off and raised the club, it looked like he knew how to use it. Donovan took another step back and took a defensive stance.

"I don't know who you are or how you are involved in any of this," Saleem growled. "But I advise you to keep your distance from me." He took another step forward with the club raised and Donovan retreated again.

Donovan raised his hands and started walking backwards. Saleem, never taking his eyes off Donovan, got into his car and gunned the engine. He spun the tires in reverse and then sped off down Gibson.

Donovan had little doubt that Saleem was at least familiar with whatever was going on with Said and Zaman that much was obvious. He doubted he would get any farther with Saleem now that he'd spooked him. His best option was to let the Feds handle it.

Sixteen

As soon as Donovan got back to his office he pulled up Decker's number and pressed dial.

"I was getting worried about you Donovan" Decker answered. "I thought you'd lost interest."

"Hardly" Donovan replied. "As a matter of fact I might have something for you."

There was brief pause and then Decker came back, "And what would that be?"

"What do you know about Qadry Saleem?"

Another pause. If he hadn't heard Decker breathing, Donovan would have thought that the connection had been lost. Finally Decker said, "He's a known associate of Tariq Zaman."

"He's more than that," Donovan replied. "He knows Amar Said and he's neck deep in whatever Said is involved in."

Decker snorted. "And how did you come to this conclusion?"

"Look asshole, I've been doing what you told me to do. I got his name from Zaman's daughter and I checked him out."

"What do you mean, you 'checked him out'?" Decker asked.

"Don't worry," Donovan said sharply. "I didn't compromise your top secret investigation. I followed a lead and now I'm passing the information on to you."

"You were supposed to get close to Zaman."

"Well, Said has effectively shut that down. This is the best you're going to get for now."

Decker exhaled and then said, "I have to run this by Captain Brown."

"Yeah, you do that," Donovan said. Then he cut the connection.

He looked down at the phone in his hand and noticed that his hand was shaking. He wasn't sure if it was from anger or fear or some combination of the two. Had he bought himself some good graces from the Feds or simply some time? He looked at the phone again; there was a text from Sherry. He took a breath and opened it.

"Check your email," was all it said.

He logged on to his Gmail account and Sherry's message was right on top in the inbox. There was no subject and when he opened it, saw that there was no message just an attachment. He downloaded the file--it took a few minutes due to its size--and then opened it.

The first few pages were the BPD file on Demetrius "Tiny" Cantrell: date of birth (which made him twenty five years old,) physical description (as Donovan had suspected the name "Tiny" was an attempt at irony, the guy weighed in at over three hundred pounds,) his arrest record (a couple of possession with intent charges and an assault,) then his mug shots, the guy staring into the camera nonchalantly, like he was at the DMV getting his license renewed.

The next couple of pages were troubling. It was a rundown of the last year or so of Cantrell's activities. Donovan recognized the format and the shorthand. Somehow Sherry had gotten her hand on intel from the gang squad. Given what Foster had told him about the current climate on the gang squad, Donovan hoped that she hadn't gone against his wishes and stuck her nose into that hornet's nest. Still he read on.

Apparently Cantrell had had some kind of falling out with the Street Kings, a gang he had been running with since he was a juvenile. A person didn't usually get to retire from the Kings. The typical outcome was either incarceration or a bullet from a rival gang. There were a few OGs still around, sort of elder statesmen, but age and wisdom, as well as the threat of going back to prison made them less active in the everyday business. Donovan wondered how Cantrell had survived crossing the Kings. The report said that Cantrell had moved out of the Masten district of Buffalo, the Kings' seat of power in their shrinking sphere of influence due to their rival NBH's expansion. He'd somehow wound up at an address on 15th Street on the city's West Side.

Damn it Sherry, Donovan thought. He should let this go. He stood up and walked to the door to the reception area. It was raining outside and the wind had kicked up, thick drops pelted the office window. A vivid image of Allison Baker's forsaken body in the garbage tote flashed through his mind. It would be dark out soon; the days were getting noticeably shorter. He went back to his laptop and plugged it into the printer. After gathering what he had printed he locked the office and went out to the Lincoln.

The rain had dissipated into a light mist by the time Donovan turned off of Hampshire Street onto 15th. It was already dark and the streetlights seemed to be struggling to cut through the gloom. He cruised as slowly down 15th as he dared. He knew the Lincoln wasn't the most ideal vehicle for a stealth mission but he had no choice. He realized too late that he had passed the address from the file Sherry had sent him. He turned right onto Massachusetts Avenue to circle the block.

Donovan hadn't spent all that much time on the West side as a cop, about a year when he was in uniform and an occasional visit when he was on the Gang Squad. During Buffalo's boom in the early part of the Twentieth Century the West side had become home to the city's burgeoning Italian-American population. In the Seventies and Eighties a wave of Hispanic immigrants made their mark in the area and then at the turn of the century a wave of asylum seekers from Africa and Central Asia had added their imprint to the mix. Like the rest of the Inner city though, as the bottom of the industrial sector had fallen out, the West side had fallen prey to the inevitable urban blight. It was one of the neighborhoods where even though there were well kept homes and civically minded people, you were never more than a couple blocks away from trouble, drugs, gangs and all the mayhem that went along with them. Before Donovan had left the police force, he'd had more than a few dealings with the Latin Kings. That made Cantrell's relocation even more puzzling. What was an ex-member of the Street Kings doing holed up in Latin King territory? Donovan had been off the force for over five years now and he realized that a lot of things could have changed, but still it was odd.

He came down 15th again and realized how he had missed it on his first pass. It was a two story house, probably single family occupancy. The bottom floor front door and window were dark and he would have thought the place was deserted except for a faint light in one of the upstairs windows. He slowed the car down and looked from side to side. The street seemed quiet, probably due to the weather. Unfortunately 15th was a one way street so he made another circle around the block and parked about fifty feet from the house.

"Okay, now what?" he asked himself. He hadn't really prepared for an extended stakeout and he wasn't about to go and ring the doorbell. He had no plan and wondered what he'd hope to accomplish. He exhaled and turned the car off. An hour went by and he felt his legs getting stiff. A few cars had passed by but there was no activity at the house. He could see the upstairs window, still illuminated by the dim light, but hadn't seen any movement. He was thinking about packing it in when a pair of headlights appeared in his side view mirror. He crouched low as a Cadillac Escalade, its windows tinted almost black, passed by. The driver pulled into

the driveway of the house and idled there. A moment later a large
man emerged from between the houses and got into the back seat
of the Escalade. That has to be Tiny Cantrell, Donovan thought.
The Caddy backed out into the street and when they were almost
at the end of the street, Donovan started the Lincoln and pulled
out. Leaving as much distance as he dared, Donovan followed the
Caddy down Massachusetts and then turned right onto Niagara
Street. He tried to be less conspicuous, putting two cars between
himself and his quarry. When the Escalade turned onto the ramp
to the I-190 north, he did likewise.

The Escalade picked up speed and Donovan kept pace with
the Lincoln, its eight cylinder engine humming effortlessly. Where
the hell are they going? He asked himself. He was able to keep two
or three cars between himself and the Caddy, hoping they hadn't
noticed that they were being followed by somebody's grandfather.

When they hit the South Grand Island Bridge, Donovan had to
scramble to pull out his wallet for the toll. The Caddy must have
had an Easy-Pass because it zipped right through in the automated
lane. Shit, he thought, he was in line behind a car with Ontario
plates and it didn't look like they were moving any time soon. The
toll collector was leaning out of the booth with an impatient look
on her face. Finally the correct currency was produced and Donovan was through the toll barrier and onto the bridge. He pressed
down on the accelerator and gradually picked up speed. He had
to weave from lane to lane a few times, once drawing the ire of
a honking minivan. He was starting to wonder if the Caddy had
exited when he saw the distinctive tail lights about a quarter mile

ahead. He'd started to suspect the reason Cantrell and company were on the Island was the same reason that most of the traffic on the expressway at this time of night was; they were cutting across to get to Niagara Falls.

Surely enough after they crossed the North Bridge off of the island, the Escalade exited onto the Niagara Scenic Parkway and into the City of Niagara Falls, New York. After a short jog on John Daly Boulevard, the Caddy turned left onto Falls Street and there it was, directly ahead of them, the opulent facade of the Casino Niagara.

The Caddy made a right onto 6th Street and Donovan slowed, not wanting to get too close. When he made the right turn he saw the Caddy turning left at the end of the block. He accelerated slowly and got to the corner just in time to see the Escalade pulling into the casino's parking ramp off of the access road that ran between the casino and the ramp. He drove past and as soon as he was sure he was out of sight, executed a three point turn and then turned right onto the access road and into the parking garage. Being a Friday night, the casino was busy and the ramp was full. Donovan guessed that the Caddy was headed towards one of the upper levels. He followed the signs towards level two. As soon as he rounded the corner he saw the Escalade up ahead, ascending the ramp slowly, looking for a parking space. On the third level the Caddy pulled into a spot and Donovan accelerated past and went around the next corner before the Caddy's doors opened. He almost ran over an elderly couple on the fourth level and finally found a spot.

He descended the two flights of stairs to the foot bridge that connected the parking garage to the casino. He spotted the distinctive shape of Cantrell and two other men on the opposite side waiting for the elevator. Donovan slowed his pace until the three men entered the elevator and then jogged to the elevator door, the elevator was headed to the ground floor. He took the stairs down to the ground floor and then opened the door slowly into the lobby. Cantrell and his companions were entering the casino's main entrance. Cantrell was in the middle, a man with dreadlocks in front of him and another man with a shaved head behind him in back, almost like he was being escorted. As Donovan entered the casino, a Native American security guard eyed him warily.

The casino floor was busy, older people playing the slot machines and the gaming tables full of determined looking middle aged and younger people. Donovan saw Cantrell and his companions making their way to the bar off to the left of the floor. When they reached the bar, cornrows tapped an African American man on the shoulder and the man turned around and looked hard at Cantrell. Donovan stopped in his tracks. The man at the bar was Calvert Fredrickson's nephew, Travis Parker.

Seventeen

Donovan had worked with Travis Parker at Travis's uncle's private investigating firm, Fredrikson & Associates. Travis' story had at first been an inspiring one, former gang banger, disillusioned by the death of his best friend, taken in by his mother's brother, employed and headed for law school. The last time Donovan and Travis had crossed paths however, Travis had put a bullet in the man's head who had killed his uncle and told Donovan that he didn't see the point of playing by the rules. Travis had arguably spared Donovan's life that night, but there was little question that he was going back to the dark side. Now here he was, consorting with a suspected murderer and gang turncoat. Donovan forced himself to move, dipping his head and looking down at his phone as he circled the bar area.

Travis was in his mid- to late twenties now. When they worked together Travis had dressed to blend into whatever situation his uncle had assigned him; jeans, hooded sweatshirts, work clothes. Tonight he was dressed in what Donovan thought people referred to as business casual, a black blazer over a gray button down shirt open at the collar. Out of his peripheral vision, Donovan saw Travis, Cantrell and the other two men start to walk away from the bar. He followed at a safe distance as the group got on an escalator to the balcony. Another security guard nodded to them as they went through a door into the attached hotel. Donovan got on the escalator and ascended to the second level. He smiled as he walked up to the Hotel entrance. As he reached for the door the security guard put a hand up and said, "Excuse me sir, are you a guest of the hotel?"

"Um, not exactly," he replied, still smiling. "I'm meeting a friend in his room."

The guard narrowed his eyes and shook his head. "You'll have to check in at the desk in the lobby." He then took a step between the door and Donovan. "This entrance is for guests only."

Donovan thought about arguing, but didn't want to set the man off. "Okay," he said backing off. "No problem." As he turned to go, he thought he heard the guard say something into his lapel microphone but couldn't make out what it was. He had to regroup. He could wait in the lobby or the garage until Cantrell and the others came out. But the meeting between Travis and Cantrell had set an alarm off in his head. What was that all about? Travis had more or less faded into the woodwork after Cal's death. The few times he had spoken to Cal's widow Grace, she'd said that she had lost contact with Travis and his mother, Sheila after Grace had moved to Atlanta to be close to her own daughter. Here he was now, taking meetings in a casino hotel.

As he made his way across the gaming floor towards the lobby a large Native American man in a blazer and tie was walking in his direction looking right at him. Shit, Donovan thought. He took a slight left but the man turned to intercept him. As he reached the last row of slot machines the two men came face to face. The man had to be at least six foot four and weigh over two-fifty and looked pretty solid.

"Yes?" Donovan said, trying to sound nonchalant.

"I need you to come with me," the man said quietly. That didn't matter though; they had already caught the attention of a few of the slot machine players closest to them.

"I think there's been a mistake," Donovan said. He made to step around the man who put up a huge hand to stop him.

"It would be better if you didn't make a scene," the man said. Donovan was eye level with his engraved name tag. It said Mr. Jimerson. Out of the corner of his left eye he spotted another guard off of his left shoulder. Sure enough he turned around and there was a third guard behind him to his right. Before he knew it Jimerson had grabbed his upper right arm with a vice like grip. "This way," was all he said.

He was taken to a small room off of the gaming floor and sat down on a bench with metal rings mounted on it for handcuffs. This must be where they brought the cheats, drunks and thieves before they were turned over to the Niagara Falls PD. Opposite the bench was a simple metal desk where Jimerson had stationed one of his guards before he left the room. The guard looked bored and only occasionally looked away from the computer monitor on the desk in Donovan's direction.   Donovan looked around the room. It was empty except for the bench, the desk and a large filing cabinet. There was a single surveillance camera mounted on the ceiling. That gave Donovan some comfort, if anything did happen to him in this room, there would be a record of it. Of course who controls what happens to the recordings?

After about fifteen minutes of silence Donovan finally said, "Can I ask what this is about?"

The guard, a young kid in his twenties with closed cropped hair that screamed wanna-be cop, said, "No idea," without looking at Donovan.

"Can I ask what we're waiting for?"

The guard finally looked at him flatly and said, "Mr. Jimerson is talking to the Director of Security."

"What? Why? I haven't done anything. Is this the way you treat all your customers?"

The kid wasn't buying the fake indignation. He shook his head and went back to the computer screen.

Ten more minutes went by and the door finally swung open. Jimerson crooked his finger at the guard at the desk and said, "Okay Cody, we're good here.

Cody shot up out of his seat and walked around the desk and to the door. As he walked through he nodded at someone out of Donovan's line of sight. Jimerson held the door open and then opened it for a man in his fifties with close cropped wiry black hair flecked with gray. He was wearing a dark blue suit and a white shirt with the collar open. He was also wearing an expensive looking pair of eyeglasses. As he made his way to the desk he said, "That will be all Clarence."

Donovan glanced at Jimerson who had a quizzical look on his face. The man in suit took a seat at the desk and looking up at Jimerson added, "It's alright. I'll call you if I need anything." Jimerson frowned at Donovan and then left the room.

He pulled a notebook and pen out of this jacket pocket and flipped the notebook open. He looked up at Donovan and cleared his throat. "My name is Anton Proctor. I'm the Director of Security for the casino." He paused and looked down at the notebook. Donovan didn't know if the silence was an act of intimidation or something else so he remained silent. Proctor looked back up at him and said. "I'm going to need to see some identification."

"Why would you need that?" Donovan asked.

Proctor raised an eyebrow. His glasses had a slight tint to them and Donovan couldn't read his eyes. "Because I'd like to know who I'm talking to and I'd like to keep this civilized," he said.

"Civilized?" Donovan snorted. "Pretty sure I've got the big guy's fingerprints embedded in my arm."

"Mr. Jimerson was only trying to make sure he got you off the floor without incident."

Donovan shook his head. "Look, I don't know what you think I've done or what the deal is here…"

Proctor put a hand up and interrupted. "We'll get to that in a moment. But first, how about you show me some ID?"

"I don't think I will until I know what this is about."

Proctor sat back in his chair and grimaced. He thought for a moment and then said. "If that's the way you want to play it." He opened a desk drawer and pulled out a form. He looked up at the camera and made a circular gesture with his right index finger.

"What?" Donovan asked.

"If you don't want to show me your ID then you can show it to the Niagara Falls Police when they arrest you for trespassing and harassment."

"Wait, aren't you guys a sovereign nation? Why get the police involved?"

"We're not on the Rez, Sir. Any laws broken have to be reported to the local police."

Donovan could feel his blood rising and he was trying to rein it in. "What laws have I broken?"

"I already told you," Proctor said as he started to fill out the blank form in front of him. "Harassment and trespassing."

"You want my ID? Fine." Donovan reached back for his wallet. The sudden movement didn't quite make Proctor flinch, but Donovan did notice him stiffen slightly. He opened his wallet and using one hand to cover up his PI license in case they were watching upstairs, he took out his driver's license and placed it on the desk. Proctor looked up at the camera and shook his head. He started writing the data from the license onto the form.

"Who exactly was I harassing?" Donovan asked.

Proctor didn't look up from the form. He answered, "We have you on our surveillance following a guest in from the parking garage and then attempting to follow him into the hotel."

"Would that guest happened to be named Demetrius Cantrell?"

Donovan got the reaction he wanted. Proctor paused ever so slightly and then looked up. "One, I don't know who that is and two, It doesn't matter who it was," he said. He went back to the form and filled in another few lines and signed it with a flourish. He stood up and put the form into a small copier on the desk and handed Donovan his driver's license. The copier whirred into life and then when the copy came out he handed it to Donovan and added, "Mr Donovan, you are barred from this property for ninety days. If you are found in the casino or the hotel you will be arrested for trespassing."

Donovan took the copy and without looking at it folded it up and put it into his jacket pocket. Proctor was already on his way to the door so he stood and followed. He realized it was a done deal so any debate would be fruitless. Proctor opened the door and Jimerson's large frame filled the opening. "Mr. Jimerson will escort you to your vehicle," Clay added flatly.

Jimerson led the way, across the gaming floor, the players still absorbed in chasing their imagined winnings. It wasn't until they reached the garage that Donovan spoke. "Nice clientele you have in there. Jimerson looked at him sideways but didn't respond.

They were almost to the Lincoln and Donovan spoke up again. "So, are you a part of this? Or just the hired muscle?"

Jimerson turned to face him. He was frowning again and looked both confused and angry. "A part of what?" he asked.

"The men I was following and the man at the bar. Do you know who they are? How well do you know your boss?"

"I think you should get in your car and go," Jimerson said taking a step towards Donovan.

Donovan stood his ground. "You're in your own little world here Clarence. But you should know that the men you are protecting can bring a lot of unwanted trouble to your doorstep."

Jimerson took another step and now was towering over Donovan, glaring down at him. Donovan was trying to read him and thought he saw a glimmer of uncertainty in Jimerson's demeanor. Jimerson finally said, "You don't know what you're talking about."

"Maybe I don't," Donovan replied, slowly fishing the keys out of his pocket. "Or maybe I just don't know everything yet. Do yourself a favor Clarence, take a closer look at the people you've got running around your casino."

Without warning, Jimerson's hand came up and he shoved Donovan hard in the chest. Donovan barely kept his balance and raised his arms. He stopped himself and raised a finger towards the Lincoln. "Get the fuck out of here. Now!"

"I'm gone," Donovan said, hands still raised. "Look me up if you want to talk."

"Not going to happen," Jimerson said as he turned to walk away.

Eighteen

"Fuck!" Donovan said to himself as he pulled out of the parking garage. He kept one eye glued to his rear view mirror to make sure he wasn't being followed and continued to do so until he'd made the next few turns. How deep did this whole thing go? Tiny Cantrell was being protected but it was more than just a bent cop on the gang squad. There Cantrell was, shacked up in a hotel room with Travis Parker and a couple of other hoods. But what was the connection between Hunter, Parker and Cantrell? Whatever it was, it couldn't be good, or the kind of thing that wouldn't bite him back if he stuck his nose into it.

He pulled out his phone and was about to call Foster when it buzzed with an incoming call.

"Hello," he said after the first ring.

"Tom?" It was Alia, and he knew right away that something was wrong.

"Where are you?" she asked. Her voice was weak and barely audible.

"I'm on the Grand Island Bridge. Alia, what's wrong?"

"I'm at the Education Center. Someone is trying to break in."

"Have you called the police?" he asked.

"No."

"Alia, listen, hang up and dial 911 and then find someplace out of sight. I'm on my way."

"Please hurry. Tom," she said and the line went dead

Donovan pinned the accelerator to the floor and the engine roared to life. He went as fast as he dared on the I-290 and the 90. It wouldn't serve any purpose getting pulled over by a trooper. Twenty-five agonizing minutes later he pulled into the parking lot of the center.

Something was wrong. If Alia had followed his instructions, the place should have been crawling with Orchard Park cops. There was only one car in the lot and it was Alia's. Donovan hesitated. His Glock was back at the apartment, locked in his gun safe. He looked at his phone and considered dialing 911. What if it was a false alarm? Alia had sounded positively terrified when she called. He climbed out of the Lincoln, pulled up her number and hit redial as he double timed it to the front entrance. It rang four times and went to voicemail. He pocketed the phone and tried the door. To his surprise, it was unlocked.

The corridor was in shadow, the only illumination coming from the emergency exit signs at the end of the hallway. To his left Donovan saw that the office door was ajar and the lights were on. He thought about calling out to Alia but he had a cold feeling come over he so he quietly walked over to the door and slowly pushed it open.

The office was empty. There was a half cup of tea on Alia's desk and a sweater draped over the back of her chair. He left the office and turned left down the corridor. As his eyes grew accustomed to the gloom he saw that a light was coming from the makeshift TV studio at the end of the hall. He quietly walked down the hallway, briefly glancing into the other darkened rooms. The door to the studio was open and he peeked around the corner into the dimly lit room.

Alia was lying on the floor in a pool of blood. Donovan stepped forward and saw that her throat had been cut. He stared down into her face which seemed to be frozen in terror, doll's eyes staring off at nothing. Next to Alia's body was a picture someone had snapped of him and Alia at the coffee shop. He fought off the bile rising from his stomach and steadied himself. He pulled out his phone and started to dial 911 when heard a noise from behind him and turned around.

Qadry Saleem was standing in the doorway with a sword in his hand. It was shaped like a machete but bigger and the blade was covered in blood. Saleem was perspiring but the look on his face was oddly collected considering what he had just done. His fierce brown eyes glared at Donovan. Donovan instinctively reached for the gun that wasn't there.

"You forgot something eh?" Saleem sneered. He had pulled out a chrome .45 with his left hand as a precaution and pointed it at Donovan.

"You fuck," Donovan growled. "Why kill her? She had nothing to do with this."

"That is a matter of opinion. Others may have thought she knew too much or was talking to the wrong people."

Donovan glanced back at Alia's body and the picture lying next to it. He felt himself getting nauseous with the thought that he had caused her death in an attempt to save his own skin. Out of the corner of his eye he saw Saleem moving towards him.

"The sword or the gun?" Saleem asked with an evil smile.

"What?"

"You choose," Saleem said, raising the sword. "How do you want to die?"

Just then there was a loud *thwap* from the direction of the doorway. Saleem's body jerked and he almost went down. He straightened up and after dropping the sword put his hand up to the side of his neck. When he pulled it away it was covered with blood.

Donovan and Saleem turned towards the door to see Katrina Bedford standing there with a pistol with smoke coming out of the attached suppressor. She was wearing a black sweatshirt with the hood pulled up over black jeans. Her face was impassive, almost blank. Saleem gurgled something unintelligible and when he went to raise his weapon Katrina put another round into the center of his chest. This time Saleem went down. With her weapon still pointed at Saleem, Katrina calmly walked over to him, kicked the gun away and shot him in the forehead.

"What the fuck?" was all Donovan could manage to say.

Katrina looked at him. "Hello Donovan," she said as she

unscrewed the suppressor and put it in her pocket. "I was just passing by and I thought I'd pop in and say hi."

"Seriously," he said, "what are you doing here?"

She still had the pistol in her hand as she walked past him. "No time for that now, she said as she bent over to pick up the photograph. "We should go."

Donovan shook his head. "No... no. I should call the cops."

She turned to look at him. "Why?" she asked impatiently. "You can't do anything for her now. Besides, you're already neck deep in this and I'd hate to see you go under."

He shook his head again but couldn't speak. He looked back at Alia.

"Come on," Katrina said. The pistol was out of sight now and she was looking at him with what? Sympathy? Donovan pocketed his phone and followed her out of the room.

They left the building and walked around the side towards the lot, Katrina setting a brisk but controlled pace. When they arrived at Donovan's car Katrina turned to look at him. "Go back to your office," she said. "I'll explain everything there. She turned and walked to the back of the lot and then disappeared between two bushes. Donovan looked back towards the darkened building and then got into the Lincoln and drove off.

Donovan didn't remember much of the ride back to North Buffalo. He could still see Alia splayed out on the floor of the

TV studio. He thought back to the last time they had spoken and how angry and frightened she had been. He had put her in danger. It was true he never expected things to get so out of hand but then again, wasn't that his M.O.? She and her father had come to America to escape that kind of senseless violence and now, because of him, she was dead. It was small comfort that Saleem was dead too. He had intended to kill Donovan too and make it look like some kind of convoluted honor killing. And now there were more questions; who was Amar Said? What had he done to provoke the government and feel the need to kill an innocent woman to protect himself? Where did Alia's father Tariq fit into it? Or more urgently where was Tariq Zaman right now? Was he dead too?

He shuffled up to the office door and was fumbling for the key when he heard a voice behind him. "Let's go Donovan. We don't want to be standing out here all night."

He whirled around to see Katrina, hands in the pocket of her sweatshirt behind him. She had seemingly come out of nowhere, noiselessly again. He turned back to the door and unlocked it.

"You live upstairs right?" she asked as they walked into the back office. He nodded and she added, "Good let's go."

Upstairs in the apartment he stood in the middle of the living room and looked at her. She had taken off the hood and was looking back at him. She was small, maybe five-three or -four and her brown hair was pulled back in ponytail. She had high cheekbones and a small nose. Under other circumstances she would be considered attractive, but there was a hardness about her brown eyes and a world weary look to her expression.

"You look like you need a drink," she said.

He started to walk towards the kitchen but she put her hand up. Then she pointed to his recliner. "Sit down, I'll get it. What do you have?"

He collapsed into the recliner. "Under the sink," he mumbled.

He heard her rummaging around the kitchen for a few minutes and then she returned with a healthy measure of Jameson's in a glass for him and a beer for herself. She sat down on the old couch opposite him and took a pull off the beer. After a moment she spoke up. "Before I tell you my story, could you indulge me on how you got involved in this?"

"Why would I do that?" he asked. He took a sip of the whiskey and felt the burn in his throat.

She smiled wanly. "Come on Donovan. You and I go back. I never did get to thank you for what you did for Donna."

"We go back, but I wouldn't say we're old friends."

"You still sore about the first time we met?" she asked. "You were creeping around my mom's back yard and Donna's life had been threatened. You think I overreacted? You're still breathing aren't you?"

"Well, thanks for that I guess."

She shook her head. "Or was it because of the dirty cop or Gary Shields? In your heart of hearts you know they had it coming."

"You get to decide who lives and who dies?" he said closing his eyes.

"Only in extreme cases. You know what it's like to feel that anger, don't you? I took it easy on your girlfriend."

"She's not my girlfriend and she was just looking out for me."

"Whatever. She's a feisty one though."

He stared at her over the glass. He was aware that she knew some of his story. Was she referring to Derrick Trent? Or some of the other people with whom he'd crossed paths? He took another drink and then told her the story; being hired by Tariq Zaman, picked up by Captain Brown and the Feds, his getting Saleem's name from Alia. He stopped there because the end of the story was too painful to put into words.

Katrina was sitting back listening and watching him. When he stopped speaking she took another drink and then said, "Okay, I'm going to tell you how the rest of us got here.

Nineteen

Anbar Province, Iraq 2006.

Another hot day in the sand box. It was over 100 degrees Fahrenheit under a cloudless sky. The heat shimmered off the asphalt as the Humvee roared up the road headed west out of Ramadi. Corporal Evans was in the back seat, to his right sat the man in fatigues without any markings or insignia. He glanced at the man occasionally. He was middle aged, too old to be active duty, unless he was an officer, which Evans doubted. He had to be a spook, CIA or a contractor. He was leaning towards CIA, because the contractors he had seen since he had been in country traveled with their own security, dead eyed ex-special forces guys, adrenaline junkies who actually seemed to enjoy being in the shit. Evans knew that the contractors made big bucks but when he was done with his hitch he would go back to Ohio and leave the Marine Corps behind. He had a month left until he rotated home and couldn't get out of Iraq fast enough. Not

that he regretted enlisting, he loved the brotherhood and camarade-
rie but had a creeping feeling they were just playing Whack-A-Mole
with the insurgents and the Jihadists.

"What's our ETA, Sergeant?" the man asked.

"We're fifteen minutes out," Sergeant Matthews yelled from the
front passenger seat without turning around.

Evans looked at Matthews, Sarge had seemed uneasy when
he'd come and told him and Cruz to gear up. He'd not said anything about where they were going and what they were doing. It
was disconcerting to say the least. Usually Mathews was a detail
guy. He made sure everyone knew exactly where they were going
as well as their responsibilities. Clearly he was unhappy about this
assignment. It probably didn't help his mood that it was just the
four of them, roaring through the desert in a single Humvee.

Fifteen minutes later they arrived at a small village. It couldn't
have been made up of more than seven or eight simple stone houses and it looked deserted.

"Is this right?" Matthews asked over his shoulder.

"This is the place," the man said, looking straight ahead.

"Where is everybody?" Evans heard Cruz ask from the driver's
seat.

"Who knows?" Matthews grunted. "Either we scared them off
or the insurgents did. It's all collateral damage."

Then, from the other end of the village a battered old Toyota
pickup approached slowly. It pulled to within twenty yards of the
Humvee and stopped. A small man with a grey beard emerged
from the passenger side and walked towards them.

"Alright," the man they were escorting said. "I need you to get out. Leave your rifles in the vehicle and give that man one of the boxes from the back."

When they had picked up their passenger at base camp, he'd had them load three heavy metal boxes into the back of the Humvee.

Matthews glanced back over his shoulder. Evans could tell none of this was sitting well with his Sergeant.

"C'mon, Sergeant," the man added. "We're in and out. We've got two more stops to go."

Matthews grimaced and then nodded at Cruz and Evans. The four men exited the Humvee.

Evans and Cruz moved quickly to the rear of the vehicle and grabbed one of the boxes. They carried it towards the pickup. As they neared the man who had gotten out of the Toyota their passenger held a hand up.

"Where is Ahmed?" their passenger asked the man.

"He could not come," the man replied. "I have come in his place."

"And you are?" the passenger asked.

"That is not important," the man said looking directly at the passenger. "Just hand over the gold and we will be done."

Evans could feel perspiration running down his face. Suddenly his gear seemed to weigh twice as much.

The passenger pulled out a Satellite phone. "I need to speak to Ahmed," he said, glaring back at the man.

"That will not be necessary," the man from the truck said as he raised his right hand.

"Ambush!" Evans heard Matthews yell from behind him. A loud burst from an automatic rifle and Evans turned around just in time to see Matthews cut down as he was trying to get back to the Humvee. Several men with automatic weapons had emerged from the houses on either side of them. "Motherfucker!" he heard Cruz say. He looked at Cruz, who was reaching for his sidearm. Another loud report of gunfire and Cruz went down. He had his hand on his own sidearm when he felt the hammer blow of a round hit his helmet and another tear into his leg.

He opened his eyes, his leg was screaming and his head throbbing. No one was speaking but there was movement around him. He slowly reached for his weapon, still in its holster. He drew it and glanced up at the man with the gray beard. Suddenly, someone stepped on his wrist, pinning his gun hand to the ground.

Twenty

"So this is about gold?" Donovan asked.

"A lot of it," Katrina replied. "Five million and change. It was intended to pay off the warlords to be more sympathetic to the cause of Enduring Freedom."

"And this Captain Brown? He's trying to recover it?"

"That will never happen. Not all of it anyway," she said standing.

Donovan thought for a moment and asked, "So where do you come in?"

"Long story short, our client, the people who put up the cash, think that your Captain Brown may not be the patriot he claims to be."

"Client? Who do you work for anyway?" Donovan slurred. Suddenly his tongue felt swollen and his eyelids heavy.

"You could say I'm a contractor too," Katrina said. She was standing over him now, looking down at him.

Donovan looked at the empty glass in his hand. "What did

you do?" he asked.

"You were in shock," she said. "I gave you something to help you sleep." She held out her hand and added, "C'mon, I'll tuck you in."

Donovan opened his eyes. The window shade was gray with the first morning light. He heard the shower running down the hall and then turn off. The events of the last night came back to him like a distant dream. He closed his eyes to try to shut them out and heard the bedroom door open. Katrina entered the room, wrapped in a towel, her medium length brown hair still damp from the shower. She looked into his half closed eyes and then dropped the towel to the floor and got under the covers. Donovan didn't remember getting undressed but suddenly she drew her warm body to his. She climbed on top of him, her body was taut and muscular but her skin was smooth and warm. Despite the drugs and the grief he became aroused instantly. It had been a while since he had been with a woman. After a few moments she pulled him on top of her. She seemed surprisingly tentative, almost vulnerable yet still passionate.

When they finished, Katrina was lying on her stomach. Donovan ran his hand down her back and felt a long scar, twelve inches maybe that ran from her hip to the middle of her back.

"Occupational hazard," she said softly, anticipating his question.

He wanted to ask so many more questions but closed his eyes instead.

The next time he opened his eyes the light on the shade told him it was mid-morning. His head ached and he felt dizzy so he went into the kitchen and made himself a cup of coffee. After a long hot shower he felt somewhat more like himself. He couldn't stop thinking about Alia and by extension Katrina.

He made his way downstairs and into his inner office. As soon as he entered he heard his mother's voice from the reception area.

"I already told you," she was scolding someone. "He's not answering his phone and I have no idea where he is."

"Mrs. Donovan, it's very important that I speak to your son." Donovan recognized the voice of Special Agent Steve Decker, one of the last people he wanted to speak to right now.

"Yes, you mentioned that," Rose snapped back." But it doesn't change anything. Now if you would like to leave a card I'll give him the message."

Donovan didn't want to leave his mother dealing with the Feds by herself, but at the same time it sounded like she was holding her own. His flight instinct kicked in instead so he turned to go out the back door. Something caught his eye as he turned, or rather something that wasn't there. He looked down at his desk, his laptop was gone. Katrina. But why? Was she shutting him out or was she protecting him? He'd have to deal with that later. Right now he had to move the boxes that were blocking the exit to the back alley.

The sun hurt his eyes as he stepped outside. Shit, he thought, the keys to the Lincoln were upstairs. Did he risk going back inside? He looked up and down the alley, checking to see if Decker had someone outside watching. He was trying to decide what to do next when the Black Escalade accelerated up the alley and stopped right next to where he was standing. The guy with the dreads from the casino jumped out of the passenger seat. He was wearing an army jacket and wrap around shades.

"An old friend of yours wants a word." the man said.

Donovan shook his head. "Now's not really a good time…"

Dreadlocks opened the jacket, revealing a 9mm tucked in his belt. "Look my man, you may be an old friend of his, and he is extending you this courtesy. Me, I could give a fuck about you. So just get in the car and don't make me have to explain why I felt an imminent threat on my own life and had to waste you."

Donovan was out of arguments so he got into the Escalade and they took off down the alley.

Twenty One

There were two other men in the car with them. Donovan recognized the man with the shaved head sitting next to him in the back as Dreadlocks' companion from the night before. There was a smaller man driving, he was wearing a dark suit with his shirt collar open and wire-rimmed glasses. No one said a word as they made their way downtown and then onto the Skyway headed south. They exited on Fuhrman Boulevard and a few minutes later slowed to a stop and parked behind a black Lexus. The man next to him looked at him with dead eyes; he knew it was a sign to get out.

Dreadlocks was already out and he motioned with his head in the direction of the metallic canopy on the other side of the bike path. Donovan walked between the neatly landscaped foliage and towards the canopy. It was still warm, by September standards, but there was a definite hint of autumn in the air. The sun was shimmering off the lake, but Donovan could make out the silhouette of two people playing chess on one of the concrete tables. Despite the weather there wasn't another soul in sight. Once under the canopy, his eyes adjusted and he saw Travis Parker staring intently at the chess pieces. His companion, who couldn't have been more than sixteen, looked up at Donovan and said, "Yo, 'T'."

Parker looked up at Donovan and gave him a slight smile. He looked back at his opponent and said, "Go wait with the others. I need to talk to this man."

"What?" the kid said with a laugh. "Just when I was on the verge of whuppin' your ass?"

"What did I tell you about underestimating an adversary?" Parker smiled back, but there was a seriousness to his voice. The kid took the hint and promptly stood up and walked quickly past Donovan towards the road.

Parker stood up. Again he was dressed in "Business Casual," a button down shirt over dark pants. "Hello Tom," he said. He didn't extend his hand nor look like he was expecting Donovan to offer his.

"Travis. Long time."

"Yes, it has been Tom. And a lot of things have changed."

The last time Donovan had seen Parker, a drug dealer had been executed and Parker had hinted that he was going into the business himself. Judging by the clothes and the cars and the entourage, business was good.

"Who's the kid?" Donovan asked, jerking his thumb back towards the cars.

"My cousin. Just trying to keep him on the right path."

"What path is that?"

Parker shook his head, "Don't be disrespectful," he said.

"Like you disrespecting your uncle's memory?"

Parker frowned, clearly becoming agitated. "You think you know me? My uncle was a decent man, always trying to do the right thing. What did that get him? A bullet in the head from some greasy Dago, who, if I remember correctly, was looking for you."

That stung Donovan into silence. Mike Manzella had set a trap for Donovan but had murdered Cal Frederickson instead when Cal had intervened.

"No, the way I see it," Parker continued, "you're either the hunter or you're the prey in this world. I decided on the former."

Donovan shook his head, finding his words again, "You had choices."

"I did," Parker responded. "Go to college, put me and my mom into a world of debt and for what? Some bullshit thirty grand a year job with no future? Nah, I have to do right by me and my own. Nobody else is going to."

"But at what cost?" Donovan asked, raising his voice.

"Humph, what do you mean?"

"Protecting a murderer?"

Parker was looking past Donovan. Donovan turned around to see Dreadlocks glaring at him with 9mm at his side.

"What? Tiny?" Parker asked. Donovan turned to look back at him. "The man's a fool, but a useful fool. When the time comes he will be dealt with."

"Travis…" Donovan started but Parker put his hand up.

"That's all I'm gonna say Tom. This is a courtesy because I

always liked you. My uncle liked you too. But this is the last time I extend this courtesy." Parker took a box off of one of the benches and started to put the chess pieces in it. "My associates will take you home."

Twenty Two

No one said a word in the Escalade on the way back from the lakeside to North Buffalo. As they turned left from Parkside onto Hertel Donovan remembered something. "Oh, you might not want to drop me off in front of my building, The FBI was there when you picked me up."

Dreadlocks whirled around from the front passenger seat, menace in his eyes. The man with shaved head next to Donovan in the back was glaring too. "You tryin' to be funny, motherfucker?" Dreadlocks asked.

"Nope, just thought I'd mention it, you know, avoid any unpleasantness."

The man with the glasses who was driving had barely reacted. He calmly pulled over to the curb and put the vehicle in park. Then he spoke for the first time, "And why would the FBI be at your office, Mr. Donovan?"

He was soft-spoken and benign looking, but Donovan noticed the other two men fall quiet and defer to him.

Donovan said, "Don't worry, it's totally unrelated to whatever you and Mr. Parker have cooking."

No one said a word for a moment. From where Donovan was seated he could only see the driver in profile. "Very well," the driver said. "You won't mind getting out and walking the last few blocks then?"

Donovan heard the door locks clip open and he put his hand on the latch. He paused and looked at the driver. "You know what this is about right?" he asked.

The driver looked in the rearview and their eyes met. He didn't answer.

"Tiny Cantrell?" Donovan pressed.

A flash to his left and then he felt the fist hit him in the jaw. He saw red for a moment as the jolt of pain ran through his head. He glanced at the man with the shaved head and braced himself for another punch. "Get the fuck out of the car," the man said instead. Donovan climbed out and waited until they had pulled away before he rubbed his jaw. He didn't want to give them the satisfaction. It was obvious though that he'd struck a nerve.

As he walked the last few blocks to Saranac Avenue he pulled out his phone and saw that he had missed three calls from Decker. He knew he'd have to call him back eventually to explain his side of things regarding the events at the Outreach center. He hadn't had time to check the internet to see what the news outlets were reporting, but it felt like the whole thing had gone to shit and he could only imagine what Decker and Brown were thinking. Not yet. He was tired and frustrated and needed time to think.

He cautiously rounded the corner onto Saranac, on the lookout for Decker or any other Fed. Instead, as he approached the office the door swung open and Kathleen Sherman, the State Tax agent emerged, struggling with a heavy looking cardboard box and her shoulder bag.

"Ms. Sherman," he said, holding the door.

She looked at him flatly, but said nothing.

"Um, could I help you with that?"

She straightened up and almost lost her grip on the box.

"No," she said curtly. "I've got it. Your receptionist has been very helpful already," she added with a hint of sarcasm. She turned and walked towards a white sedan parked at the curb.

Donovan entered the office as Rose was pulling on her coat. "What was that all about?" he asked.

Rose picked up her bag and put over her shoulder. "I gave Ms. Sherman some of the things she requested and a number of things she didn't," she said.

"What?" Donovan asked.

She looked at him and smiled faintly. Still, he couldn't help but see the sadness and disappointment in her eyes. "Don't worry," she added. "Just enough to keep her busy for a while until you figure this out.

Donovan stood there speechless. Rose walked up and looked him in the eye. "Tom, I'm not stupid. I've been around this family long enough to know what's what. I know Hugh left you money."

He went to speak but she held up her hand. "You're a grown man and I'm not going to lecture you on right or wrong, but I know, no I pray, that you intend to do the right thing here."

"Mom…"

She shook her head. "Don't," she said. "No explanations Tom. Just figure it out." She brushed past him and went out the door. Donovan went into the inner office and plopped down in the chair in front of where his laptop used to be. The knot in his stomach made him forget the pain in his jaw.

———————

He sat there for some time. Eventually realizing that he had to do something, anything to extricate himself from the mess he was in. He pulled up Decker's number and hit the dial button.

"About time," Decker said as a greeting.

"We need to talk."

"Oh you think so?" Decker replied. "Is your mom tired of running interference for you?"

"Not Brown, just you and me."

He could hear Decker breathing on the other end. Finally Decker said, "Do you know how deep in theshit you are?"

"I have a pretty good idea."

"Zaman's daughter is dead. Zaman's missing. The guy you thought you were tipping us off about is dead in the same room. And you pick this time to go off radar?"

"I know all of that," Donovan replied. "I was there."

"What?"

"I was at the Outreach center last night."

"Fuck!" Decker yelled into the phone. "Stay where you are. We're on our way."

"That doesn't work for me," Donovan replied. He put the phone on speaker and pulled up his list of contacts. He sent the list to the wireless printer on the corner of his desk.

"Donovan!" Decker was livid.

"I'll call you." Donovan replied. He ended the call and took a letter opener out of the top drawer and pried off the back of his phone. He removed the memory card, put it in his pocket and then left the phone on his desk. He got up and quickly left the office.

Twenty Three

7:30 PM and it was already dark. The temperature had dipped into the fifties and the breeze carried the hint of even cooler temperatures. Donovan pulled the dark hoodie over his head and crossed Fillmore into Martin Luther King Park.

When he'd called Decker on his brand new, prepaid cell phone he'd told him to come alone or he would bolt. He doubted Decker would follow his instructions but he wanted at least a slim chance of not getting hauled in again. He cut left onto the ring road that circled the enormous wading pool, now drained and closed for the winter and walked along the tree line. Decker was standing by himself at the edge of the wading pool. Donovan emerged from the shadows and whistled. Decker turned towards Donovan, his coat undone and his hand on the butt of his Smith and Wesson .40. Donovan held up his hands and said. "Relax, it's me."

Decker drew his weapon but didn't raise it. "Lift up your sweatshirt and turn around." He hissed. Donovan did as he was told and then said, "I come in peace."

"Can't be too sure with you Donovan. A lot of people who cross your path seem to turn up dead."

"Fuck you Decker," Donovan shot back. "I was at the Outreach center but I had nothing to do with it."

"What? 'Wrong place, wrong time'?"

Donovan shook his head. "Alia called me last night. She said that someone was trying to break in. When I got there she was dead."

"And Saleem? I suppose you found him dead too?"

"Yes," Donovan lied. Against his better judgement, something told him to leave Katrina out of his story for now.

"So why run? Why not be a good citizen and call it in?

Donovan looked at Decker for a beat and then said, "I think I was being set up."

Decker snorted. "Set up by whom?" he asked.

"Saleem. It was supposed to look like an honor killing. The Muslim woman and the Infidel."

Now Decker hesitated and frowned. "So who executed Saleem?"

"I don't know, and I wasn't going to stick around to find out. Judging by the way you're acting I think I made the right call."

Decker half raised the weapon. "Give me one reason I shouldn't bring you in right now as a material witness."

"Because I already told you everything I know. And locking me up won't get you any closer to Said" Donovan said.

"I suppose you're going to tell me you can still help us with that in spite of the fact that you seem to have fucked this up royally."

"I think I might," Donovan replied. Waves of guilt and regret washed over him as the picture in his mind of Alia's dead body flashed before him.

Decker paused for a moment and then holstered his weapon. "You have forty eight hours to make something positive happen. After that, I'll let Captain Brown work his magic on you."

Decker turned to leave but Donovan called out. "How well do you know Brown?"

Decker half turned back towards him, "What?"

"Your Captain Brown. What do you know about him? He's not FBI is he?"

"No. Not that it's any of your concern."

"CIA?"

"What are you getting at Donovan?"

"Just curious about Brown's hard-on for Said," Donovan shrugged.

Decker frowned and said, "All I know is he had NSA and Homeland Security clearance. My unit and I were seconded to the investigation of Said."

"You might want to ask him if he's crossed paths with Said before."

Decker turned fully now and took a step towards Donovan. "I'm going to ask you one more time. What the fuck are you implying?"

Donovan raised his right hand to stop Decker. Suddenly a red dot, a laser pointer from an unseen sniper, appeared on his chest, directly over his heart. Donovan slowly looked up from the dot to Decker. "I see you have trust issues Decker. Maybe you should check your own house first."

Decker shook his head and said, "Forty-eight hours asshole." Then he turned and walked off in the other direction. The red dot was gone and despite the chill air, Donovan could feel the sweat run down his back.

Twenty Four

Donovan parked the car a half block from his office on North Park. He pulled the hood up and made his way to the back door in the alleyway. He knew that he couldn't stay in his apartment for the time being. Too many people knew where he lived. He would send his mother a text in the morning, telling her to steer clear of the place until she heard from him. He worried that she would be even further upset but at the same time didn't want to take any chances. He hugged the wall in the alley, his head on a swivel, looking for anything or anyone out of place. Once he was inside he made his way upstairs and pulled an old duffel bag out of the closet. He grabbed a few changes of clothes, some toiletries from the bathroom and finally his Glock from the gun safe. Outside, after one more check down the alley, he hurried back to the Lincoln.

A half hour later he had checked himself into the Stay-More Motel on Niagara Falls Boulevard, paying cash. There were only two other cars and a work van in the lot in the center of the courtyard. He stretched out on the cheap, lumpy mattress and tried to sleep. He opened his eyes and stared at an odd stain on the ceiling. The room felt small and stuffy and he kept picturing Alia lying in a pool of blood, her large brown eyes staring off into nothing.

He thought about Allison Baker lying in a garbage tote. The sole connection was himself. Why did everything he touched seem to turn to shit? Eventually, exhaustion took over and he drifted off into a restless sleep.

He stirred several hours later. Daylight was seeping in on the edges of the window blinds. He checked the time on his burner phone. It was 7:12 AM. He sat up and took out the printed list of contacts from his pants pocket and called Bob Stanley's cell phone. He knew Stanley was usually in his office early before he went to court and he hoped Stanley would answer even if he didn't recognize the number on his caller ID. It went to voicemail. Donovan cursed under his breath and then left a message, telling Stanley it was urgent and to call him back on the new number.

Donovan had stripped down and turned on the shower when the phone vibrated on the edge of the bathroom vanity.

"Tom, what the hell is going on?" Stanley asked in lieu of a greeting. Donovan could hear a level of anxiety behind the lawyer's usually calm, neutral tone.

"The Zaman thing," Donovan replied. "This is a lot more than some xenophobic graffiti."

"What do you mean?"

Donovan decided it was time for full disclosure, "Said and Zaman are up to their eyeballs in something shady that happened in Iraq. Stolen gold worth enough for Said to decide that Alia was expendable."

He heard Stanley exhale down the line. "Shit," Stanley said. "I had the sense that Zaman was holding something back but I had no idea."

"Have you heard from Zaman?"

"Not since last week."

"I need to talk to him."

"I tried to call him yesterday but his phone has been disconnected." Stanley replied. He exhaled again. "One of the things that should have raised a flag is he gave me an email address to use if an emergency came up. I could kick myself for not reading more into it."

"I didn't see it either Bob, but here we are. Could you try to contact him and have him call me?"

"Will do. Jesus Tom, are you in trouble?"

"Not yet," Donovan lied. "I'm just taking precautions. I just want to get his side of the story. He probably knows it already, but tell him his life may be in danger."

"If he's not dead already," Stanley said, following Donovan's reasoning.

After Donovan showered, he wiped the steam off the mirror and looked at himself. There were more flecks of grey in his dark brown hair than he remembered and circles under his eyes. Here he was, holed up in a cheap motel with a burner phone, a gun and a borrowed car. "You really stepped in it this time," he said to his reflection.

He'd managed to piss off the Feds, an Iraqi warlord and one of the city's most notorious gangs, all within a few days' time. He knew he couldn't sit idly waiting for Bob Stanley to find Zaman. He thought about going to the Fillmore Market to confront Said, but what good would that do? He could always work on his other problem, Tiny Cantrell and Travis Parker. He went to the nightstand and dug James Foster's card out of his wallet.

It turned out Foster had been taken off suspension but as Foster had predicted he was off the Gang Squad and was currently on "administrative duty" at BPD headquarters on Franklin Street. Foster had reluctantly agreed to meet Donovan a few blocks away from Police HQ at Niagara Square.

The meeting was scheduled for 10 AM. Donovan arrived a half hour early, concerned he wouldn't be able to find a parking spot nearby. He found a public lot not too far from City Hall and found himself at Niagara Square with twenty minutes to spare. The sun was out and the weather had warmed. He could have done without his jacket except that he was carrying the Glock in a holster on his belt.

Niagara Square had been in existence since the early 19th Century, where it had been part of the original street design of the Village of New Amsterdam. It was still the nexus of Downtown Buffalo, where Delaware Avenue, Court Street, Genesee Street and Niagara Street all intersected. In the middle of the square stood a monument to President William McKinley, who had been assassinated by a self-proclaimed anarchist, Leon Czolgosz at the Buffalo Pan-American Exhibition in 1901. It was quiet in the Square, the only other person seated at a bench was a homeless woman with a small wire shopping basket. It was too early for the lunch rush. The only activity seemed to be the people coming and going from City Hall on the west side of the Square.

Donovan was tired, but too keyed up to sit. He spent the remaining time pacing around the outskirts of the Square, waiting for Foster's arrival. 10 AM came and went and Donovan wondered if he was being stood up. Another ten minutes went by and he pulled his phone out of his pocket and was about to call Foster.

"Hey," Donovan heard from behind him. James Foster was approaching, dressed in a coat and tie and wearing wraparound sunglasses, the sun gleaming off of his mocha colored scalp.

"I've got ten minutes," Foster said. "I'm on a tight leash."

"That's fine," Donovan replied. "I just have a couple of questions." Outwardly, Foster seemed calm, but there was something in the way he stood rigidly that told Donovan he was uneasy. "Do you know who Tiny Cantrell works for?"

"I told you already, the NBH."

"No Foster, I mean who specifically in the NBH?"

Foster frowned behind the dark glasses and said, "We had two or three names near the top of the food chain..."

"No," Donovan interrupted. "There's one name. Travis Parker."

"Bullshit!" Foster snorted. "The kid who used to work for Cal Fredrickson?"

"Yeah, his nephew."

"Urban legend Donovan. There were rumors about a new

Don but Parker's name never came up in anything we had on the NBH."

"That's because he's smart and careful. But trust me, I have first-hand knowledge that he's the man at the top now."

Foster didn't reply, he just stared. Donovan pressed on, "So you're telling me that Lt. Hunter and the rest of the gang squad are in bed with Travis Parker and The NBH?"

"What am I supposed to think?" Foster hissed. "I got too close to something and next thing I know, I'm off the gang squad and pushing papers in this monkey suit," he said as he tugged at his tie.

Donovan looked at Foster, trying to read him. Finally he asked, "Who was in charge of the gang squad before Hunter?"

"Why do you ask?"

"Humor me."

"Anton Proctor." Foster said.

"What happened to Proctor?"

"Retired. He put his twenty in and took a job with the Indians up in the Falls."

"No shit?"

Foster was becoming agitated. "What do you mean by that?"

"Travis Parker is taking meetings at the Casino up there, and Proctor is running interference in his role as Director of Security."

Foster took a step towards Donovan and lowered his voice. "Fuck you man. I don't know where you get off, but Tony was good police. Of course what would you know about that?"

Donovan stepped closer too. Foster had a good four inches on

Donovan but Donovan met his gaze without flinching. "It's a hell of a set of circumstances, isn't it James? And it begs the question; how well did you know Proctor?"

"Fuck you!" Foster spat.

Donovan took a step back. "If you're clean on this then save yourself James. Otherwise you'd better cover your ass or a suspension will be the least of your problems."

"Fuck you again," Foster growled. He started to say something else but bit it off then turned and walked away.

Twenty Five

Donovan was sitting in the Lincoln, wondering what to do next when the burner buzzed in his jacket pocket. He pulled it out and saw Stanley's private number on the caller ID.

"Zaman is alive," Stanley opened with.

"Where is he?" Donovan asked.

"Tom, he is genuinely terrified. Before I tell you where he is he wants you to know he had nothing to do with Alia's death. He thinks Said is tying up loose ends and he thinks he's next."

"How deep is he involved with Said?"

"He's involved to a point, but he didn't get into specifics. Apparently Said has something on him and was blackmailing him."

Donovan thought for a moment and then asked, "And you believe him?"

"I do, as far as what he told me so far. He's afraid to go to the authorities because Said still has some kind of leverage. Alia was part of it but there's more that he wouldn't tell me."

"I need to talk to him," Donovan said.

"That's good, because he wants to talk to you."

"Why me?"

"He told me that Alia trusted you and said that you could help them."

A new knot formed in Donovan's stomach.

Stanley continued, "Zaman said he tried to keep her out of it and now he blames himself for what happened.

Plenty of blame to go around, Donovan thought. "Where is he Bob?"

"I'll text you the address," Stanley said. "Like I said, he's terrified Tom, and for good reason. I could understand if you didn't want to involve yourself further in this."

"I'm already up to my chin in this. Text me the address."

———

Shortly after sunset, Donovan found himself back on the West Side, turning right off of West Delavan onto Congress Street. He drove down the one-way street, lined with trees and 1940s era two family houses until he saw the address he was looking for. He found a parking spot halfway down the block, pulled in and killed the lights. He pulled up the sweatshirt hood and climbed out of the car, checking up and down the block for movement. The temperature had dipped into the fifties, so windows were closed and the block was eerily quiet. He patted the Glock on his hip for reassurance and walked up to the house. Up on the front porch he rang the doorbell on the far right door, the one for the upstairs flat. The hall light flicked on through the glass and he saw a woman descend the stairs. She was in her fifties and had dark skin and graying dark hair pulled back off her face. She flipped a switch and the porch was illuminated by a naked bulb over the door. She seemed nervous and Donovan realized he still had the hood up. He took it down and held up his hands. She considered him for a moment and then opened the door a few inches and peered up at him but said nothing.

"My name is Donovan, I'm here to see Tariq."

She hesitated for a few seconds and then flipped the porch light off and opened the door. Donovan checked the street behind him one more time and followed her upstairs. The woman gestured him into the dining room in the middle of the flat and then disappeared into the kitchen. Donovan could smell the remnants of dinner, something highly seasoned. His stomach growled but he pushed the sensation off.

A moment later Tariq Zaman emerged from the darkened kitchen. If Donovan had any doubts about Zaman's guilt or complicity with Said, they were erased as soon as he saw him. Zaman looked devastated. He had a five o'clock shadow and his clothes were wrinkled. He had dark circles under his bloodshot eyes. He looked at Donovan directly and asked, "You were there? You saw what they did to my daughter?"

"Yes."

Zaman's eyes started to fill up. "He is an animal."

"Said?" Donovan asked.

Zaman nodded. "Yes, but that is not his real name."

"Who is he?"

"His name is Mohammad Nazir. He was an officer in the Republican Guard under Saddam. When the Americans came, he slipped into the desert with some of his men and a cache of weapons, changed his name and reinvented himself as a tribal warlord. It was a ruse and he changed allegiances with the shifting winds. His only allegiance is to himself and accumulating wealth anyway he could. After my son-in-law was killed he sought me out and said he would pay me enough to get myself and my daughter out of Iraq. We are Sunni, Mr. Donovan, and the sectarian violence was becoming unbearable even before Alia lost her husband."

Zaman paused and looked down so Donovan prompted him, "What did Nazir want in return?"

Zaman looked back up at Donovan. "I owned a wholesale grocery business. The warehouse had been burned to the ground but we had managed to save three of the delivery trucks. Nazir gave me money to bribe our way out in return for smuggling something across the Syrian border."

"The gold?"

"I didn't know it at the time, but yes. I was desperate to get Alia out of the country before I lost her too." At that Zaman shook and choked slightly. "I'm sorry," he said. "Now she is gone and I have nothing. Nothing but the hate in my heart for Mohammad Nazir and the wish to see him punished."

Donovan considered Zaman for a moment. Although he was relieved that Zaman hadn't blamed him, at least partially, for Alia's death he felt his stomach tying itself in a knot again. "I may be able to do something about that," he heard himself say.

Zaman shook his head. "Mohammad Nazir is a very dangerous man. He will stop at nothing to protect himself."

"I'll be careful. Just promise me you'll stay out of sight until I contact you."

Zaman took a step forward and extended his hand. "Mr. Stanley was right about you," he said. "You are an honorable man."

Donovan shook Zaman's hand. The compliment made him feel worse.

The woman walked Donovan down the stairs and held the door open for him. He nodded at her and as he walked past her she spoke up, "You will help Tariq?"

Donovan turned towards the woman. She was looking up at him expectantly. "I'm going to try."

She put her hand to her chest and said, "Tariq is a good man. I lost my husband and sons in Iraq. He helped my daughter and me escape six months ago." She paused and blinked something back. "He just did what he thought was necessary."

Donovan didn't know what to say so he just nodded, pulled the hood back up and left.

A few hours later and two miles away, the Escalade pulled into the driveway of the house on 15th Street. The man with the dreadlocks, Levon, turned off the engine, looked in the mirror at his passenger and said, "Wait here."

"Sho' 'nuff boss," Tiny Cantrell said from the back seat.

The man with the shaved head in the front passenger seat turned and stared at Cantrell. "Shut your mouth, fat man."

Cantrell pulled a wounded look. "I don't think my brother would appreciate you talking to me like that," he said.

"Your brother is the only reason I ain't put a bullet in that fat ugly head," the man with the shaved head replied.

"Kenny," Levon said. "Let it go."

"Yeah Kenny, mind your manners," Cantrell said mockingly.

Kenny started to say something but Levon put a hand on his arm. "Just wait here," Levon said quietly.

Satisfied that the situation was at least temporarily defused, Levon climbed out of the Escalade and walked up to the front porch. He unlocked the door and deactivated the alarm, then waved back to the Escalade.

Once the three men were inside the house Levon reset the alarm.

"I'm hungry," Tiny said.

"Of course you are," Kenny shot back.

Levon shot Kenny a look and then said, "There's some pizza in the refrigerator."

"Shit man," Cantrell whined. "That shit's two days old."

"Man, this ain't the fuckin' Hyatt," Kenny said.

Cantrell shot Kenny his best tough guy stare and then said, "Fuck you man."

Levon stepped between them and said, "It's that or nothin'."

Cantrell snorted and turned towards the stairs. Once he had ascended the staircase Levon looked at Kenny. "Why do you let him get to you like that" he asked.

"Fat piece of shit," was Kenny's response. He turned and walked back towards the kitchen.

Upstairs Cantrell opened the bedroom door and flicked on the light. He took two steps towards the bed and heard the door shut quietly behind him. He turned around and said, "What the fuck?"

She was standing there, a girl, no a woman. She was small, maybe five foot three, wearing a black sweatshirt over black jeans and tactical shoes. She was staring at him, expressionless, except for the piercing brown eyes.

"What the fuck" he sputtered again.

She held a finger up to her lips. He noticed her other hand was shoved deep in the sweatshirt pocket. "Let's not get your friends downstairs upset."

Cantrell was starting to perspire. "Who the fuck are you?"

She smiled without warmth. "What's wrong Demetrius? I thought you liked petite women."

He frowned. "I don't know who you are lady, or what the fuck you want. But one word and my boys downstairs will come up blasting."

"Fucking pussy," she laughed. "I figured as much. I weigh a buck-thirty. What do you go, about three-fifty?"

Cantrell glared at her in disbelief for a moment and then said. "I'll wipe that smile off your face, bitch."

He lurched forward and went for her neck. Before he knew what happened the knife was out of her pocket and struck him under the left armpit. His momentum carried him into the door as she stepped aside. He spun around as fast as he could but she was right there. The black combat knife in an overhand grip. The knife flashed three more times, striking him in his chest and torso, each strike finding arteries. He collapsed to his knees, arms at his sides. He could feel himself going into shock. The woman stepped forward. "I thought you liked it rough too," she almost whispered. Then with one more slash she severed his jugular vein.

Levon was downstairs, sending a text on the extra phone he was carrying when he heard the thud from upstairs. He put the phone away. Cantrell was a noisy motherfucker but the noise was odd, like Cantrell had fallen or something. "Shit," he said to himself. At the top of the stairs he saw that Cantrell's door was shut and it was deathly quiet. He thought about calling out to Cantrell or downstairs to Kenny but then thought he was being paranoid. The house had been sewn up tight and a few payments to Latin Kings, the gang whose turf 15th street was in, meant that all should be well. Just to be sure he pulled the Smith and Wesson out of his belt and held it at his side as he pushed the door open. "Cantrell," Levon called. The room was deathly quiet with a palpable static in the air. Levon brought the pistol up into a two handed grip and stepped into the room.

On his third step he slipped on something wet. Just as he was on the verge of regaining his balance he felt the kick in the back of his knee. The knee buckled and he went down on all fours, barely keeping his grip on the gun. He realized that he was in a pool of blood and his heart was pounding. He pushed himself up into a kneeling position and braced himself for another blow. Instead he felt someone grab him by the dreadlocks and pull something sharp across his throat. He felt the cold air enter the open wound as the life started to ebb out of him. He tried to turn around to face his attacker but whoever it was shoved him hard, face down on the floor. He had put his hands up to his throat in a futile attempt to staunch the flow of blood and laid like that for a moment. A small pair of boots came into his line of vision, dimly illuminated by a light in the hall. He tried to speak but could only gurgle the word, "...cop."

Kenny was standing in front of the microwave, waiting for the timer to go off for the piece of pizza he was reheating when he heard the first thud from upstairs. He shook his head at the thought of Cantrell crashing around like the oaf that he was. The timer went off and he took the pizza out of the microwave and carried it to the kitchen table. He heard two more thuds. "Motherfucker," he said out loud. He put the pizza down and walked into the living room. He had just started to climb the stairs when the women rounded the corner to make her way down.

"What the fuck" he said. The woman raised a silver handgun that looked like the one that Levon carried and shot him in the chest with a loud bang. Kenny fell onto his back, defenseless since he had left his Baretta on the kitchen table. The woman was walking past him, just out of reach, when she stopped and pointed the gun at his forehead. She fired once and then dropped the gun from her gloved hand. She calmly walked to the door, deactivated the alarm and disappeared into the night.

Twenty Six

Donovan parked the Lincoln on Fillmore and walked quickly towards the Market. He stole a glance up at the building across the street where Decker and company had been watching Said/Nazir the previous week. The apartment was dark again with no movement or telltale glint off of a camera lens. Where they still there? Had they set up shop somewhere else? It didn't matter now. He felt he had to make a play to bring on some kind of resolution.

A buzzer sounded when he opened the door and walked into the market. The same man, who he recognized as Nazir's driver from the other day, was behind the glass at the register. The man looked up from the magazine he was reading, his bored look replaced by something hostile when he recognized Donovan. He stared daggers at Donovan and said nothing.

"I need to speak to Nazir," Donovan said.

The cashier shook his head. "There is no Nazir here," he said.

Donovan smiled and looked towards the door at the back of

the market, out of the corner of his eye he saw the cashier reaching for something under the counter. Donovan turned back towards the cashier and opened his jacket, revealing the Glock on his hip. "Relax pal, I've got one too. Besides, what are you going to do? Shoot me through the Plexiglas?"

The cashier didn't move nor did he bring his hands up from under the counter. Donovan took a card out of his pocket with his left hand, his right hand on the butt of the Glock. He pushed the card through the opening on the counter and said, "Whatever. Tell Nazir to call the number on the back of the card. Tell him I can help him with his problem."

The cashier didn't take his eyes off Donovan to look at the card. Donovan took a few steps backwards and reached for the door handle. "Have a nice night." He said and then pulled the door open.

Another glance over at the apartment across the street and Donovan made his way back towards the Lincoln. Still no sign of life, but that didn't mean he wasn't being watched. If he was, he hoped he would have enough time to explain his plan to Decker. Right now he had to keep moving. As he climbed into the car and turned the key he felt the burner buzz in his pocket. He put a few blocks between himself and the Fillmore Market before he fished it out and saw that he'd received a text message.

It was from Bob Stanley and said, *call your friend, she said it's urgent.* Stanley was cautious enough not to use names and Donovan could appreciate that. It had to be Sherry. She was the only female in his circle who would know enough to use the lawyer as an intermediary. He put a few more miles behind him and, satisfied that he hadn't been followed, pulled over and punched in Sherry's number. She answered it on the second ring.

"Oh hey Dad," she said. Donovan could hear voices in the background. She had to be at the precinct. "Can I call you back in about ten minutes?"

"OK…" Donovan started but then the line went dead. He was parked on Genesee Street near Goodyear Avenue. The area seemed deserted with only an occasional car driving by. After ten minutes the quiet was starting to get to him and he was just about to start his car when the phone buzzed.

"What the hell is going on?" Sherry asked.

"What do you mean?"

"You haven't heard? Tiny Cantrell is dead."

"What?" Donovan gasped.

"You don't know anything about it?"

Donovan's mind was racing. He was staring out the windshield at nothing but the empty street. Sherry's voice brought him back, "Tom, I don't know what happened but Ray Hunter from the Gang Squad is losing his mind. They pulled James Foster in an hour ago and word has it they're looking for you too."

"Sherry, I swear I had nothing to do with it."

"You know I believe you but why would Hunter even know who you are?"

Donovan wracked his brain for a moment and then came up with the only possible answer.

"I followed Cantrell up to the Falls the other night."

"Shit," she said. "Do you think they were following Cantrell too?"

"Not according to what Foster thinks. If anything Cantrell's new boss tipped Hunter off."

The line was quiet for a moment and then Sherry asked, "Who is Cantrell's new boss?"

"Travis Parker."

"What? Travis? Cal's nephew? No fucking way."

"It's true Sher," Donovan replied. "I had an unscheduled meeting with Travis the other day. He's near the top of the food chain in the NBH. He made it clear to me that Tiny was under his protection for the time being."

"I know you said he went to the dark side, but shit. He was just some intern at the firm a couple of years ago."

"I know. But he told MIke Manzella that he'd swung some deal with some outfit out of Chicago right before he put a bullet in his head. He's smart and he's focused and he may not be the head of the NBH, but I'm thinking he's close to the top."

"Tom, I am so sorry," Sherry said.

"For what?"

"I pushed you into this."

"You didn't push me into anything, Polack. It always bothered me that nobody ever answered for what happened to Allison Baker. After Foster came to me with his conspiracy theory I was all in."

"Shit," Sherry blurted. "I didn't tell you the worst part."

"It gets worse?"

"There were two other bodies in the house with Cantrell. Rumor has it one of them was a cop."

"What? A cop?"

"One of Hunter's guys was apparently deep undercover in the NBH. He and Cantrell had their throats cut and the third guy was shot in the heart and the head.

Donovan was dumbstruck. A cop? Was it one of the men who he'd dealt with the other day?

"Tom, you still there?"

"Yes."

"What are you going to do?"

"I don't know," he answered. Things had gone to shit in ways he'd never imagined they could.

"Let me bring you in."

"What? No!" He was aware he'd raised his voice. He took a breath to calm himself and continued, "I'm toxic right now Sher. You need to keep your distance."

"Better it was me than if Hunter or his people find you first!"

"I mean it Sherry. I'm going to figure this out. I just need some time."

"Dammit Tom…" she started, but he had already ended the connection. He was considering ditching the phone but he was waiting, and hoping, for Nazir to call. If any of the people who had his number were being monitored they may be able to trace the burner. He just had to hold on to it for a little while longer.

Twenty Seven

With nothing to do but wait, Donovan was making his way back to his motel room. He was exiting I-290 onto Niagara Falls Boulevard when the phone buzzed, the incoming number blocked on the caller ID.

"Donovan," he answered.

"Tell me what you want?" asked the heavily accented voice on the other end.

"Nazir?"

"No, I am the one you spoke to at the market."

"I need to talk to Nazir," Donovan snapped.

"We shall see about that, my friend. First, you mentioned that you could help my employer with his situation. What did you mean?"

Donovan was going to argue, but he knew he was pressed for time. "Tell your employer that I can bring Zaman to him."

A moment of silence and then the man came back, "What does that have to do with my employer?"

Donovan bristled, "Listen asshole. Tell Nazir that Zaman is ready to go to the authorities. The only thing stopping him is me."

"Again, I ask you how this is our concern?"

"You guys overplayed your hand when you killed his daughter. He has nothing to lose."

Silence again. Donovan looked at the phone wondering if the man had hung up. Then he heard his voice, "We will call you," the man said and then broke the connection.

"Fuck!" Donovan said out loud. He hoped he had Nazir's attention.

He pulled into the parking lot of the Stay-More motel and killed the lights. After he was satisfied that he hadn't been followed or was being watched, he climbed out of the Lincoln and entered his room.

In the bathroom he brushed his teeth and splashed water on his face. He stripped off his jacket, placed the phone and his Glock on the nightstand and stretched out on the bed. All he could do now was wait. His head was starting to ache so he closed his eyes.

He thought about Cantrell and the dead cop. He knew Cantrell probably had a price on his head from his former associates in the Street Kings, but if they didn't know where he'd been tucked away by Travis Parker how would they get to him? It wasn't their style either, two stabbings and one executed by gun. The Kings would have gone in guns blazing and laid waste to the whole house. Then there was the stolen laptop with his emails and case notes. Katrina had resources beyond his comprehension and she was a stone cold killer. All signs pointed to her. But why? She was after Nazir and the stolen gold. What did she care about the man who killed Allison Baker?

Donovan hadn't intended to fall asleep and had no idea how long he'd been out, but the next thing he was aware of was a loud crash as something hit the door then the sound of wood splintering and metal twisting. His initial reaction was to reach for the nightstand and the gun. Bright lights his eyes and large shadows entered the room.

"Police! Don't move!" someone barked from behind the lights. Donovan froze with his palms up. Hands grabbed him roughly and rolled him onto his stomach. He was cuffed and held down.

"Bathroom's clear!" he heard a voice yell. Someone flipped on the light and he was yanked to his feet. He blinked, his eyes still blurry from sleep and adjusting to the light. He was surrounded by five members of the Town of Amherst SWAT team, their faces unreadable behind their visors. One of the team leaned out of the broken door and said, "We're good to go Lieutenant."

Three men walked in, plainclothes cops with Kevlar vests over street clothes. The two younger ones walked up on either side of Donovan and grabbed an arm. The older cop walked up and stood about a foot away from Donovan. He was solidly built, with close cropped dark brown hair, a five day growth of beard flecked with gray and piercing blue eyes. He had a two inch scar near his left eye. "Tom Donovan," he said. "I'm arresting you on suspicion of the murder of Demetrius Cantrell, Kenneth Johnston and Detective Devon Dixon. You have the right to remain…"

Donovan was trundled into the back of a Ford Expedition with tinted windows. He was sitting awkwardly, with his hands cuffed behind his back but given the mood in the car, he declined to complain. The older cop was seated next to him staring straight ahead and he looked pissed. It had to be none other than Lieutenant Ray Hunter from the Gang Squad.

They made their way down I-290 and picked up the I-190 South. Donovan thought they were taking him downtown to HQ. A few miles in however, the driver suddenly exited the freeway onto Niagara Street. Donovan shot Hunter a look and Hunter looked back at him with a simmering rage in his eyes.

"Where're we going?" Donovan asked, glaring right back at Hunter.

"Shut the fuck up," Hunter hissed. Then he looked away.

A few minutes later the SUV made a right towards the river and drove all the way to the end of the road. They had arrived at Tow Path Park, a marina on the southern branch of the Niagara River where it split around Grand Island. Donovan looked at Hunter again and noticed his weapon was in his lap. Donovan's door was yanked open and he was pulled unceremoniously from the vehicle. The marina was deserted, most of the boats having been put in storage for the winter and the weather too cold and unpredictable for a sane person to go out on the Upper Niagara River. Again, with one of the younger cops on each arm, he was marched to the low fence that separated dry land from the rushing black water. The cop on his right kicked the back of Donovan's leg and he fell to his knees onto the asphalt. Hunter entered Donovan's field of vision from the right side, his gun still out and down at his side.

Donovan looked up at Hunter and Hunter said, "Give me one reason why I shouldn't put a bullet in your fucking head."

"I didn't do it," Donovan replied, trying to keep his voice calm.

"Interesting," Hunter sneered. "It wasn't the Street Kings or the Latin Dons, so that leaves you as the only one who's been hanging around making a pain in the ass out of himself."

Donovan shook his head and said, "I was following Cantrell, that's all."

"Why?"

"Did you ever hear of an Allison Baker?" Donovan replied.

Hunter frowned. "I know who Allison Baker was. And I know Cantrell was probably the one who did her."

"And got away with it," Donovan interrupted.

"No shit!" Hunter came back. "You don't think I believe that piece of shit deserved what he got?" Now Hunter shook his head. "You're missing the big picture Donovan. One of my guys was inside the NBH and now he's dead."

"Listen. First I had no idea he was a cop. He basically abducted me at gunpoint the other day. And second, I wasn't there Hunter. I didn't do it!"

Hunter suddenly brought the gun up and pointed it at Donovan's temple. "Bullshit," he said. "I know all about you Donovan and your vigilante streak."

"You know what? Fuck you Hunter."

"I was undercover Narcotics when you killed Derrick Trent

and the DEA guy and I thought 'that's some shit luck right there.' But now I'm starting to see a pattern here Donovan.

"It wasn't me." Donovan said through gritted teeth.

"Do you know how long it took and what my guy had to go through to get into the NBH?" Hunter paused for a moment and held up his free hand as if waiting for an answer. Then he went on, "Of course you don't. I know you were in the gang squad but you guys were just putting a Band-Aid on things. We were brought in to make a difference."

"Like what?" Donovan asked. "Running your little private army out of the Fillmore station?"

Hunter glared at him for a moment and said, "Oh that's right, you've been talking to Foster."

"Who seems to have some valid concerns."

"My ass!" Hunter spat. "Foster's lucky to still have a job after taking a swing at me." Donovan noticed he had lowered his weapon back to his side. He was also taken aback. Foster had not included the swing at Hunter in his story. Hunter continued, "Foster was too close to my predecessor and couldn't be trusted. I don't think he knew what Tony Proctor was up to but we couldn't take a chance. Foster didn't get it and when we froze him and Proctor's other guys out he snapped. The idiot still thinks Proctor walks on water."

Donovan was trying to process what Hunter was saying and then suddenly it all made sense. Proctor retired and took a job at the Casino and then next thing you know, Travis Parker has set up a base of operations there. It's secure and somewhat off the grid. It all works if one hand is washing the other. "Who else knows about Proctor?" Donovan asked.

"Some of the brass had their suspicions," Hunter replied. But Procter had a good arrest record and was kind of a local hero. East Side born and bred and all that community policing bullshit."

Donovan considered Hunter. On one hand, he seemed jaded and bitter. On the other hand, he was deeply committed to what he was doing and the loss of a colleague was always painful. He was starting to see some truth in Hunter's version of events. Donovan then considered his theory about Katrina Bedford as Avenging Angel. While it was true she had more or less saved his hide at the outreach center, he knew firsthand she didn't hesitate when it came to spilling blood. She had also killed a cop, not a bent cop as he originally may have thought but a guy who had probably sacrificed everything going deep undercover for the job.

"Look," Donovan said. "Believe it or not, it wasn't me. But I think I know who did it."

"Really," Hunter said skeptically. "And who would that be?"

"Her name is Katrina Bedford, or whatever she's calling herself these days."

"Who the fuck is she? And how do you know it was her?"

"It's a long story, but she works for some shady security firm. She's in town trying to recover some stolen money."

Hunter raised the pistol again. Donovan looked straight into the barrel. "You know this sounds like utter bullshit, right? One woman took down two gangbangers and a cop who survived eighteen months at Gowanda to establish his cover?"

"Yes, I know it sounds like bullshit. But trust me when I tell you I've seen firsthand the kind of havoc she can wreak. She is cold blooded except when it comes to a soft spot she has for abused women."

"But why Cantrell?" Hunter interjected. "What's her connection to Allison Baker?"

"She's tied up in something else I'm working on." Donovan hoped he didn't have to go into the whole other mess he was wrapped up in. "She stole my laptop and I'm pretty sure she hacked my phone. And then, like I said, she really has a hard-on for predatory males."

Hunter lowered the gun and looked at Donovan. "How do I find her and mostly, why should I believe you?"

"That is a problem. She's basically a ghost. But I've seen firsthand that she's dangerous as hell and won't hesitate when it comes to killing. As far as believing me, that's up to you. But it's the truth. And if that's not good enough, do what you have to do. I'm tired and frankly right now I'm in deep enough shit that you'd almost be doing me a favor. What I'm counting on now is the fact that you're a good cop and you're going to do the right thing."

"Don't be so sure," Hunter said, slipping his finger off the guard and putting it on the trigger.

"Like I said, it's up to you," Donovan replied. He looked away from Hunter, through the fence at the black, rushing water. Despite the situation, he felt at peace, like a large weight had been taken off his shoulders. No one spoke for a moment, the only sound was the river rushing by.

"Stand up," Hunter finally broke the silence. The cops on either side of Donovan helped him to his feet. Hunter nodded at the cop on Donovan's right and the man started to undo the cuffs.

"Bobby, grab his stuff," Hunter nodded to the other cop.

Bobby came back from the Expedition with Donovan's Glock and pre-paid phone in evidence bags and handed them to Hunter.

Hunter held the bags out and said, "I've got the number for your burner. When I call you answer. One of the neighbors on 15th saw a woman hanging around the house a few hours before Dixon and the others were killed. I'm still having a hard time believing you're as innocent as you say, but for the time being you're free. If you hear from this ghost of yours, you call me." He held out a card. "And if I find out you're lying I won't be so forgiving next time. Understand?"

Donovan nodded and Hunter and associates turned and walked back towards the Expedition. "So, you're just leaving me here?"

"You've got a phone," Hunter said over his shoulder. "Call an Uber." He opened the door and added, "Oh, you might want to get a less conspicuous ride than that Town Car. The motel manager had a police scanner on and spotted you right away."

Twenty Eight

The overnight desk clerk at the Stay-More Motel was sound asleep when he thought he heard the buzzer for the outer reception door. He sat up in the recliner and brushed cigarette ash off of the old cardigan he was wearing and then wiped a little drool off his chin. The buzzer went off again letting him know he wasn't imagining it. "Jesus, keep your shirt on," he said mostly to himself. This time of night the clientele was usually a couple engaged in some type of low rent hookup. He wasn't here to judge, it was an easy job and he got paid off the books so it didn't jam him up with the Social Security office. He froze when he walked out of the back office into the reception area. The guy he'd called the cops on earlier was standing outside the door getting ready to press the buzzer again.

They made eye contact and the guy smiled without a trace of warmth. "It's OK," Donovan yelled through the glass door. "Just a big misunderstanding."

The clerk didn't move. After he called the cops with a description of the Lincoln the god damned SWAT team had rolled in, smashed down the door and dragged the guy away. Now here he was, wanting to come in and do God knows what. It was bad enough that he was going to have to tell the owner about the battered down door in the morning.

"Seriously," Donovan implored. "I would have done the same thing in your shoes. But it's fine. I just need my stuff." When the man still didn't move, Donovan pulled out Hunter's card. "If you want, call this guy. He's a big deal with the Buffalo Police."

The old man squinted at the card. Donovan doubted he could see the card at this distance but he was relieved when the old man stepped to the counter, reached below and buzzed him. The clerk pushed Donovan's keys across the counter and stepped back. "They said they'd send a tow truck out in the morning," he said nervously.

"Like I said," Donovan replied. "Everything is fine. And the rest of my stuff?"

"In the trunk."

Donovan reached into his jeans pocket and produced a roll of bills. He pulled a hundred off the roll and put it on the counter. "That should cover my stay," he said.

"What about the damage to the door?"

"Wasn't me, pal," Donovan answered, turning to leave. "You'll have to take that up with your friends in the Amherst PD."

The first thing Donovan had done when Hunter had left him by the side of the river was rip open the evidence bag with the phone to see if Nazir had called. He hadn't which was both good and bad. It was good that he hadn't missed the call but bad because he wasn't sure if Nazir was going to take the bait at all.

He knew he'd worn out his welcome at the Stay-More. He thought about going home but then realized that if the cops had suspected him of being involved in the death of Tiny Cantrell, maybe Travis Parker did too. Travis had warned him off and Donovan hoped that Travis knew he wouldn't do something so rash. Still he felt that going back to his office was too great a risk. The last thing he wanted to do was to put someone like his mother or Sherry in danger by reaching out for a place to crash. He thought of the one person who wouldn't bat an eye to help him out if he was in trouble.

Thirty minutes later, Donovan was in South Buffalo. He turned off South Park Avenue into the narrow driveway that ran alongside the bar that still bore his family name. The current owner, Whitey Brennan was waiting at the back door.

Donovan climbed out of the Lincoln. "Sorry to drag you out of bed at this hour," he said.

Whitey shook his head, "No worries, lad." He handed Donovan two sets of keys. "Help yourself to whatever's in the cooler. And there's the keys for the car." He gestured towards the older Saturn that was parked by the dumpster. "No rush on bringing it back. Jimmy Flannigan left it here until he's settled his bar tab, and I don't anticipate that happening anytime soon."

"Um...Okay," Donovan said, pocketing the keys.

"You want me to get rid of the Lincoln?" Whitey asked.

"Yes...I mean no," Donovan replied as he realized Whitey

meant get rid of it permanently. "It's a loaner from Anthony. Can you just stash it somewhere for a couple of days?"

"Absolutely. And Tommy, if there's anything else you need you call me, you hear?"

Donovan was going to tell him that he felt bad enough asking Whitey for this favor, but he knew it would be pointless to argue. He offered his hand. "Will do. And Whitey, thank you."

"No worries Tommy. I'd best be getting home before Connie thinks I'm stepping out on her" Whitey said with a smile.

Whitey drove off in the Lincoln and Donovan turned to let himself into the bar's back door. Suddenly he was gripped by fear. Travis Parker had warned him to stay away from Tiny Cantrell. If Travis thought Donovan was responsible and couldn't find him, would he target someone else to get back at Donovan? The NBH was not known for holding back when came to sending messages. The easiest target for a message would be his mother. "Shit," he said to himself. He jogged over to the Saturn and got in.

Twenty five minutes later he was parked on Norwalk Avenue in North Buffalo, a half block from the home Rose shared with her husband Anthony. He had allowed himself one stop, at an all-night convenience store to pick up two cans of Red Bull. The car reeked of stale beer and cigarettes but Donovan didn't mind. He wasn't going to let the shit he'd involved himself affect Rose any further.

He knew the house had an alarm system, he'd seen it himself. But beyond that he had no idea how safe they were. Anthony had done time in prison for manslaughter years ago for a youthful prank that had gone horribly awry, and as a convicted felon was legally prohibited from owning a gun. It was after 3 AM and the street was quiet. If only he had some way of reaching out to Travis and pleading his innocence.

With the adrenaline finally wearing off and exhaustion taking over he dozed off. He didn't know how much time had passed when he was startled awake by the burner buzzing on the passenger seat next to him.

"Hello," he grunted.

"Mr. Donovan?" asked a voice with a thick middle- eastern accent.

Donovan sat up. "Nazir?" he asked.

"No, it is Amar Said. I don't know who this Nazir is."

Donovan snorted and then said, "Okay, whatever you're calling yourself these days. But you called me so I guess you're interested in hearing my proposal."

A pause and then, "What is your proposal?"

"I can bring Zaman to you."

"I had hoped you would have been wise enough not to involve yourself further in things that didn't concern you," Nazir growled.

"Well, it's too late for that, isn't it?"

"You have been warned…" Nazir started.

"Yeah, I have been warned," Donovan interrupted. "I saw what your man did to Alia. I know you're desperate."

"You are overestimating your position."

Donovan chuckled. "Saleem said something similar right before I killed him."

He waited for Nazir to respond, and when he didn't he continued, "I know what you're capable of and now you know I'm not intimidated."

"You are making a mistake, Mr. Donovan."

"I may be, but what you have to ask yourself is, do you want Zaman or not?"

"Why would you bring Zaman to me? What do you get out of it?" Nazir asked.

"I know about the gold, and before you deny it you should know this whole thing is about to blow up in your face. The FBI and your old friend Captain Brown are closing in on you so here's my suggestion, take my offer, Zaman for fifty thousand US dollars and leave town while you can."

"When can you make this happen?" Nazir asked flatly.

"Tomorrow night, at a mutually agreed upon place."

Just then a pair of headlights coming from the other direction were doing a slow cruise down Norwalk. Donovan froze for a moment and crouched down in his seat. He almost missed Nazir saying, "We will call you." The line went dead.

The dark sedan drove twenty yards past Donovan's position and and executed a three point turn. Then passed him again and drove slowly past the house. Donovan sat up and started the Saturn. He watched as the sedan pulled into a spot halfway down the block. Without turning on his headlights Donovan pulled out of his parking spot and gunned the engine. He raced down the street and slammed on the brakes stopping right next to the sedan, effectively blocking the driver's side door. A young black male was in the driver's seat, staring at Donovan wide eyed. Donovan saw movement from the sedan's passenger seat and immediately was out of the Saturn with the Glock drawn and pointed over the roof of his car. Another young black man was climbing out of the passenger seat and was reaching into the waistband of his pants.

"Don't!" Donovan barked at the man, aiming the 9mm at his chest. "Put your hands on top of the car!"

"What the fuck?" the man said.

"Do it! And tell the driver to put his hands on the wheel."

The man just glared at him so Donovan prodded, "Five, four, three…" He took aim.

"Fuck this…" the man hissed.

"Two…"

"Alright," the man said. He put his hands up on the roof of the sedan. Donovan slowly circled the front of his car, never taking his aim off the passenger. He saw that the driver had complied and had his hands on the steering wheel. Donovan peered past the driver, looking to see if there was anyone else in the car. When he was satisfied there was no one else, he walked up behind the passenger and stuck the gun behind the man's ear.

"Tell your boss I didn't kill Cantrell," he said as he found the pistol the man had in his waistband. He stuck it under his belt.

"Man, you fucked up," the man said.

"Yeah, people keep telling me that," Donovan said, pressing the barrel of his gun into the man's skull. "Tell Parker I need to talk to him. You," he said, glancing in at the driver. "Take your piece out with two fingers and drop it out the window."

The driver stared at Donovan nervously. He couldn't have

been more than nineteen or twenty. "Do you think I'm fucking around?" Donovan asked. "Parker threatening me is one thing, but make a move on my family? You think I give a shit about your friend here?"

The driver reached inside his coat with his thumb and forefinger and pulled out a silver .32. He slowly rolled down his window and dropped it with a clatter onto the pavement. Donovan stepped back. "Now get the fuck out of here and tell Parker to call me."

The passenger turned around and shot Donovan a hard look. He opened the door and climbed in. Just as he was about to pull the door shut Donovan yanked it open and posted the gun at his head. "You'd better write this number down…"

When the passenger had put Donovan's temporary number into his own phone and closed the door, Donovan walked back around to the Saturn and backed it up a few feet. The sedan pulled out and tore off down the street. As soon as they turned the corner, he got out and retrieved the .32. He got back into the car and wiped the sweat off his brow. "Fuck," he said to himself.

Twenty Nine

With his message sent to Travis Parker, Donovan returned to his apartment on Saranac. He parked the Saturn down the street and walked slowly towards the building all the time looking for anything or anyone out of place. When he got to the office door he found it padlocked, with the door's original lock having been broken open. He walked around to the alley and let himself in through the side door. His office and the reception area had been ransacked. He went upstairs and found his apartment had been searched top to bottom as well. Was it the Feds or the Buffalo PD? It didn't really matter at this point he thought. It was after 5 AM and he was exhausted. He double locked the apartment door and stretched out on his bed with the Glock within easy reach.

9:30 AM and the phone buzzed. Donovan took it off the charger and answered it,

"Yeah."

"Mr. Donovan," Nazir said on the other end. "I will agree to your terms."

"Very well. 8 PM then?"

"Yes. You will bring Zaman to the market."

"No chance," Donovan snapped. "In case you didn't notice the Feds are watching you from an apartment across the street"

"You are joking."

"I am not. I'll pick the place."

"This is unacceptable."

"Tough shit," Donovan replied. "You think I'm going to let you and your goons set me up like those Marines in Iraq? Call this number at 7:45 and I'll tell you where to go."

Nazir started to say something but Donovan had already ended the call. His run-in with the NBH from the early morning hours was still fresh in his mind. He dialed his mother's number and she picked it up on the third ring.

"Mom, it's Tom."

"I didn't recognize the number. You're lucky I picked up."

"It's a long story," he answered.

"What's going on Tom? Are you alright?"

"I'm fine ma. I just wanted to tell you that things will be back to normal in a day or so."

"I can always tell when you're lying," she said. "That and I went by the office this morning and saw the padlock."

"Mom! I asked you to stay away from the office."

"Don't worry, I didn't stop," Rose said, her voice rising. "I was just curious to see if my son was still among the living."

Donovan exhaled. "One more day mom, I swear, and I'll be

in front of this thing. In the meantime, I'm begging you to stay home."

"Jesus Christ…" Rose said. Donovan knew she was crying and felt all the worse for it.

"It's almost over," Donovan said, not quite believing himself. "I have to go. I love you mom."

Rose didn't reply. Donovan waited for a few seconds and ended the call.

He had to get ready for his meeting with Nazir that evening, which left him with little time to watch over his mother. He had to slow Travis Parker down somehow, distract him. He had to hit him where he lived. He took Ray Hunter's card out of his jacket pocket and dialed the number.

Clarence Jimerson had just started his shift at the casino. It wasn't a bad job; the pay was decent and so were the benefits. He'd spent fifteen years with the Seneca Nation Marshals and had seen his fill of trouble--domestic disputes, drunk and disorderly and overdoses. When his friend Bill Littlejohn retired and went to work at the casino he told Clarence that it beat the hell out of breaking up fights or passing out speeding tickets in freezing weather. Clarence put his application in and was hired shortly after. Two years later, due to his integrity and experience in law enforcement he was promoted to shift supervisor. He knew the money from the casinos was helping the tribe, but there were some things about the business he found unsavory, like the gambling addicts and lowlifes the place attracted. For the most part, he had decided to accept the good with the bad.

After checking with his guards and their various posts he spotted Anton Proctor finishing up a conversation with one of the pit bosses by the craps pit. Clarence intercepted him as he turned to leave.

"Hey boss, you got a minute?"

Proctor looked up at him. "I was just on my way upstairs to surveillance. What can I do for you Clarence?"

Proctor kept walking so Clarence followed. "I was thinking…" Clarence started to say and then paused.

"Thinking what?"

"I want in."

Proctor broke stride for a moment and turned to look at Clarence. "Want in on what?"

"I think we should talk about this in private."

A few minutes later the two men were climbing the stairs to the second level of the parking garage. They hadn't said a word to each other on the way over. Clarence could tell Proctor had become agitated but was trying to hide it. When they reached the top of the stairs Proctor turned to face Clarence with his palms up. "What?" He said.

"Like I said, I want in."

"You want in? Into what?"

Clarence peered down at Proctor and said, "Whatever you and your friends in the hotel have going on."

"I don't have a clue…"

"Don't embarrass yourself Tony. I know who they are and what they do. I also know they wouldn't have set up shop here if it wasn't for you."

Proctor's mouth tightened and he shook his head. "You don't know what you're talking about big man."

"You've already got me doing your dirty work, like running that PI out of the building the other night."

"There are some things you don't understand."

"There are a lot of things I don't understand," Clarence shot back. "But I understand that if you want me to keep my mouth shut it's going to cost you."

"You ungrateful son of a bitch," Proctor spat. "If it wasn't for me you'd still be driving around the Rez locking up drunks."

"Maybe. Or maybe we'd have a casino without drug dealers and murderers running their business out of it."

Proctor laughed suddenly. "Look at you," he said. "I always knew that 'gentle giant' thing was just an act. You got some balls on you, my friend."

"I don't need much. I'm thinking a thousand a week."

Procter nodded and then said, "Very pragmatic of you. Well, on one hand, we could go ahead and do that. On the other hand, did you ever stop to think that the people I'm doing business with might not like an outsider making demands?"

"Are you threatening me?"

Proctor grinned. "You bet your ass I am," he said.

"Unbelievable," Clarence said, shaking his head. A set of tires chirped from the level below.

"What's that?" Proctor asked.

"You were a cop."

"So were you. Yet here you are, trying to extort a narcotics ring. So what of it?"

"Asshole," Clarence muttered.

"What…" Proctor turned towards the sound of a dark SUV racing up to their position and slamming on the brakes. At the far end of the ramp a second car, this one with its blue and red light bar flashing, came around the corner headed their way.

"Motherfucker," Proctor said as he looked up at Clarence.

Clarence just shrugged. Proctor took a step towards the stairwell but Clarence reached out and grabbed him by the collar of his suit coat. Proctor tried to shrug the coat off but by that time Clarence had pulled him into a bear hug. Proctor kicked backwards, aiming for Clarence's instep but missed. The next sensation he had was the air being squeezed out of his lungs as he was lifted off the ground and then body slammed onto the garage floor. Pain shot through his wrist and knee, the two points that had struck the pavement first.

"Easy chief," one of the four cops from the SUV yelled at him as they fanned out around Proctor.

"Watch that 'chief'" shit," Clarence said, stepping backwards.

"Oh, yeah, sorry," the cop replied.

Ray Hunter holstered his weapon and took out his cuffs. "Thanks," he nodded to Clarence. "We got everything." Hunter went over to where Proctor was still laying. "Anton Proctor, I'm arresting you on conspiracy to distribute narcotics and aiding and abetting a criminal enterprise."

He put the cuffs on a grimacing Proctor and read him his Miranda rights.

A cop from the second car came up with a radio in his hand. "Lieutenant," he said to Hunter, "we got into the hotel room. Three suspects and plenty of weapons."

"Parker?" Hunter asked.

The cop with the radio shook his head.

Thirty

"Are you sure about this?" Donovan asked for the third time.

"I am," Tariq Zaman replied. "I don't care what happens to me. I just want to look that animal in the eye one more time and curse him for what he did to my daughter."

Donovan turned the ignition and pulled away from the curb. Zaman had been quiet on the phone when he'd called that afternoon to propose his plan, but to Donovan's surprise, Zaman had agreed immediately. Now Zaman seemed stoic, resigned to whatever fate awaited him. The sun had set over an hour before when Donovan called Nazir.

He gave him the location for the meet, an abandoned lot off of French Street and added, "The first sign of trouble and we leave, and I turn Zaman over to Brown and the FBI." Nazir grunted his assent and ended the call.

At 8 PM Donovan pulled into the lot of the boarded-up business on French Street, a few blocks away from the Milkbone plant at the corner of Genesee and Fougeron. There was only one entrance to the lot, surrounded by a six-foot-tall chain link fence topped with barbed wire. Donovan drove to the far end of the lot and turned around to face the entrance then killed the lights. A moment later the same small SUV that Donovan had seen Nazir and his driver in at the outreach center, pulled into the lot. "Keep your eyes closed," Donovan said to Zaman. "Try not to move. And whatever happens, do not get out of the car." The other car drove up to within twenty yards of Donovan's position and the driver turned off the headlights.

Donovan climbed out of the Saturn, arms at his side with his jacket open. The temperature had dipped into the forties, the air was crisp and still. Nazir and the cashier from the market climbed out of the SUV. Neither of them had weapons visible and the cashier was carrying a bank deposit bag.

"Tell Zaman to come out," Nazir said.

"I can't," Donovan shook his head. "He's drugged. Do you think he'd come willingly to meet with you?"

The cashier looked at Nazir who was frowning at the Saturn. Donovan went on, "All you have to do is hand me the bag and he's all yours." He glanced past Nazir at the gate to the parking lot. Nazir picked up on it and put his hand on the cashier's arm.

"Are you expecting someone, Mr. Donovan?"

"No," Donovan lied. "I just want to get this over with without any fuck ups."

The cashier looked around nervously, but Nazir just stared at Donovan, assessing him. He withdrew his arm and nodded to the cashier. Just as soon as the cashier took a step towards Donovan, the sound of footsteps came from behind Nazir's SUV. The cashier turned around, dropped the bank bag and was reached into his coat. He was too slow. Captain Brown drove the butt of his AR-15 into the man's forehead. The cashier crumpled to the ground. Donovan reflexively was reaching for his own weapon when Brown stepped behind Nazir and shouted, "Don't."

Donovan froze and then Brown went on. "Pull it out with your thumb and forefinger, drop it on the ground and kick it away!"

Donovan complied and then raised his hands. Brown pushed Nazir and then said, "Get Zaman out here, now!"

Donovan glanced back at Zaman, who was staring wide-eyed at them. He motioned for Zaman to get out of the car. Zaman tentatively climbed out and walked up next to Donovan with his hands up.

"Where's Decker?" Donovan asked.

"You don't think I know what you're trying to do," Brown growled. "He and his team are right down the street, waiting for my signal. But first, Mr. Nazir and I have some unfinished business."

"About the stolen gold?" Donovan asked.

Brown glared at him over Nazir's shoulder. "You really don't know when to stop do you?"

Nazir was smiling. "Can you steal something that is already stolen?" he asked.

Brown pressed the muzzle into Nazir's back. "Shut the fuck

up…" A shot rang out, striking Brown in the thigh. He grunted and spun towards the source. Two of Nazir's men had entered the gate with handguns and were firing at Brown.

Nazir dove to the ground. Donovan looked at Zaman, wild-eyed and frozen in place. Donovan leapt on top of Zaman, knocking him to the ground. Donovan covered Zaman's body with his own. If anyone didn't deserve to die tonight it was him.

Nazir's men were firing wildly at Brown. Brown brought his weapon up and let a short burst fly. The gunman to his right went down but the man to his left kept firing. Brown took a round to the chest and toppled over backward. The surviving gunman yelled something in Arabic and Nazir slowly started to rise to his feet.

A muffled crack echoed off the surrounding buildings and the front of the gunman's head exploded. Nazir froze where he was standing. Katrina Bedford emerged from the shadows, clad in black with a scoped rifle aimed at Nazir.

"Give me the key," she demanded.

"What?" Nazir asked.

Donovan noticed Brown rolling over on his side. Brown grabbed the AR and was rolling back over.

"Katrina!" Donovan yelled as Brown was sitting up.

Without hesitation she turned to Brown, raised the rifle and with another *CRACK,* she shot him in the forehead. Nazir turned to run. He hadn't made it ten feet when Katrina shot him in the back.

Donovan rolled off Zaman, who sounded like he was mumbling a prayer. There were sirens in the distance. Katrina walked over to where Nazir lay and with the rifle pointed at him, rolled him over with her foot. Nazir's eyes were open and blood was coming out of his mouth.

"He's dead," Donovan said. "Now how will you find the gold?"

"I already know where the gold is, silly," she said mockingly. She bent over and ripped Nazir's shirt open. "I just need this." She pulled a chain from Nazir's neck and held it up. "This key is for a safe deposit box far away from here." She looked at Donovan. "Oh Tommy…"

Donovan had pulled the silver .32 he had taken off the gang banger the previous night from where he had taped it to his leg.

"Drop it," he said.

"I thought we were friends."

"You killed a cop!"

She shrugged. "He didn't tell me that." She raised the rifle.

Donovan fired and Katrina's body jerked. She straightened up and let a round go. It struck the ground in front of him, spraying dirt and gravel towards him. With his legs he pushed himself back towards Zaman, firing twice wildly as he did. Through the smoke he saw she had disappeared.

Zaman was hyperventilating. Donovan knelt over him and checked to see if he had been hit. Zaman was fine, just scared witless. Tires squealed as a Black Chevy Tahoe roared into the lot followed momentarily by a marked Buffalo Police car. Donovan stood up, dropped the .32 and raised his hands. Two more BPD squad cars pulled up to the gate and stopped.

Decker was the first one out of the Tahoe, gun raised. Three other agents climbed out, one of them going to head off the locals with his ID held high. Decker swept the scene, looking at Brown and then Nazir. He turned his weapon towards Donovan and walked towards him. "What happened?" he asked.

"I tried to warn you, didn't I?"

Decker shook his head. "You've still got no proof that Brown was dirty."

"Why do you think he had you stand down while he took care of business?"

"We'll get back to that," Decker said. He was right in front of Donovan and looked him in the eye. "Did you shoot him?"

"With that," Donovan said, pointing towards the .32. "Nope. And if you don't believe me just watch the video from the camera mounted on my dashboard. The shooter went that way," Donovan added, pointing towards the lot behind them. One of the other agents walked over and looked at the ground. "There's a blood trail," he said. The agent followed it to the fence with his weapon drawn. "Got a hole in the fence here," he added.

Decker frowned and holstered his weapon. "Morris, go with Clinton. Follow the blood trail and for God's sake be careful."

Thirty One

Anbar Province, Iraq 2006

Corporal Evans knew he had been hit bad. He felt the searing pain in his left arm and a cool dead feeling in his lower back. He couldn't move his legs. He blinked away the sweat and dust from his eyes and reached for his sidearm. He snuck a look up as he pulled the pistol and saw the man with the gray beard not more than fifteen feet in front of him. If he was going to die today he was going to take this son of a bitch with him. He slowly swung his arm up and was ready to aim it the bearded man when suddenly his arm was pinned to the ground by a black tactical boot. Evans looked up at the owner of the boot. It was Captain Brown.

"Sorry son," Brown said, pointing his Desert Eagle .45 at the Marine. "It wasn't supposed to happen like this."

Evans looked up at Brown in disbelief. "What have you done," he rasped.

Brown aimed and fired, the bullet struck Evans in the temple, killing him instantly. Brown whirled towards Nazir. "What the hell is going on?" He lowered the Desert Eagle to his side. He knew if he even raised it in Nazir's general direction he would be gunned down immediately.

"The plan has changed," Nazir said.

"What?"

"Ahmed was a fool," Nazir continued. "He was going to distribute the gold among men who did not deserve it. Men who could not be trusted."

"And you can be trusted?" Brown asked.

"To a point. I know you were expecting to be paid for betraying your own government, but that plan has changed as well."

Brown sighed. "And how has that changed?" he asked, tightening his grip around the gun.

"We will let you live if you do not resist. First you will hand over your weapon."

Brown glanced around. He was surrounded on all sides by men with weapons pointed at him. He dropped the weapon to the ground and one of the men swooped in and took it.

"Goodbye, Captain Brown," Nazir said as he turned towards the pickup truck.

Brown turned around towards the Humvee. One of the men was pulling the radio out of the Humvee. The man stepped back and dropped the radio on the ground. He then raised his weapon and emptied a clip into the Humvee's tires and interior. Two other vehicles drove into view from the other side of the village and the men climbed in and followed the pickup back in the direction it had come from.

When they were gone, Brown surveyed the scene, the three dead marines and the shot-up Humvee. He was shaking, not from fear, but from anger. He would find Nazir and get his pound of flesh if it was the last thing he did.

Thirty Two

Donovan was put into the back seat of the Tahoe. A white van pulled up with the rest of Decker's team and then a moment later the BPD patrol supervisor pulled up in a blue and white SUV and began arguing with Decker, gesturing effusively towards the crime scene that the locals were being kept out of. The two agents, Morris and Clinton returned empty handed. Decker looked at Clinton who just shook his head. Katrina had escaped, for now. Donovan was pretty sure he'd miraculously hit her with his first shot from the cheap pistol he had pulled. How bad was her wound? How far could she get?

Decker jumped into the driver's seat of the Tahoe and slammed the door. He had his phone pressed to his right ear and said, "Yes sir, we're on our way." He gunned the engine and pulled through the gathering of Feds and local cops, still engaged in their jurisdictional pissing match.

Fifteen minutes later they were in the underground garage of the Downtown Federal Building. Donovan had questions but reading Decker's demeanor he thought it best to keep his mouth shut for the time being. They took the elevator to the fifth floor and Decker led him to a small interview room. Once inside Decker motioned for Donovan to take a seat at the table, opposite a video camera on a tripod. Decker walked over to the side of the room and crossed his arms in front of his chest.

The door opened and two men in almost identical dark suits walked in. The man in front was African American, middle-aged with broad shoulders and a grim expression. The second man was white, probably in his thirties and was carrying a folder.

The middle-aged man looked at Decker and said, "Steve, why don't you come over here and take a seat."

Decker looked from the middle-aged man to Donovan and said, "I'd prefer to stand, sir."

The man shot Decker a look and then turned his attention to Donovan. "Mr. Donovan," he started, "I am Special Agent in Charge Walter Harris." Harris took a seat across from Donovan and took the folder the other agent had been carrying. The other agent stepped to the camera and Harris said, "That won't be necessary, John."

Harris opened the file and started to go through the pages inside. He looked over at Decker and said, "This is some bullshit, Steve."

Decker's face reddened. "Sir, with all due respect…"

"I know," Harris interrupted holding a hand up. "You were just following orders like you were trained to do. I had my doubts about this going in. This Brown guy with his NSA clearance, using you and your men like his own secret police squad."

"Those orders you're talking about came from pretty high up," Decker bristled.

"I get that, but I've been doing this long enough to know when someone smells as bad as Brown did, something isn't right. You guys froze us out from the get-go, all in the name of 'national security,'" Harris made finger quotes in the air. He shook his head and went on, "There's rules, and then there's rules son. If you want to survive in this profession you have to be more discerning."

Decker held his hands up. "I don't know what you want me to say."

"I don't want you to say anything," Harris said. "Right now I want you to go to my office with John and wait for me."

Agent John walked over to the door and opened it. Decker looked from John to Harris to Donovan. His shoulders sagged and he turned to follow John out of the room.

After the door had closed Harris looked at Donovan. "Mr. Donovan," he started. "Why don't we begin with you explaining to me how you came to be involved in all this?"

Donovan cleared his throat and then told his story, being hired by Zaman and then recruited under duress by Brown to flush out Nazir. He left out a few details, mainly his dealings with Katrina Bedford. When he finished he noticed Harris was looking across the table at him with his eyes half closed.

"I didn't trust Brown," Watson started. "Didn't know anything about him except he was ex-special forces and worked for one of the more notorious contractors in Iraq. I don't know who he knows or who he is blackmailing in the government, but Decker isn't exaggerating when he said that it's somebody pretty high up."

"Where does all this leave me?" Donovan asked.

Watson sat forward and said, "That's an interesting question. It's going to take some time to sort this out."

"You mean sweep it under the rug."

"No, that is not what I mean," Watson snapped. "I guarantee heads are gonna roll. It just might not make it into the papers."

Donovan regretted provoking Watson. He did not have an ally in the whole sordid affair. Watson seemed like a straight shooter and Donovan knew what it meant to go up against the bureaucracy. "Look, I don't care about any of that," he said. "I just want out from under this, that's all."

Watson seemed to lose some steam and sat back again. "I don't know where this is going to go or what the fallout is going to be," he said.

"And I'm willing to cooperate in any way I can."

Watson nodded. "I would hope so. Right now, I would just ask that you keep this to yourself."

"Absolutely," Donovan nodded.

"Just in case," Watson said rising, "we'll be holding on to your throw down piece, the one you winged the shooter with."

"Fine." Donovan stood as well.

Watson walked up to him and offered his hand. Donovan shook it.

"I had my doubts about you too, Mr. Donovan," Watson said. "Maybe I still do. On the surface though it seems like you were trying to do the right thing. If you hadn't forced Brown's hand who knows where we'd be."

"I was, I guess," Donovan replied. Not like he'd had much choice.

Harris hesitated and then said, "As a token of our gratitude, is there anything I can do to compensate you for your cooperation?"

"Take care of Tariq Zaman. He's not entirely innocent, but he's been through the wringer."

"Watson nodded and said, "If he cooperates, Mr. Zaman will be offered a place in witness protection."

"I have a feeling he's ready to cooperate."

"Anything else?"

Something from the back of his mind came to Donovan. "There is a slight problem you can help me with."

Thirty Three

Two days later

T hings were slowly being restored at the office. Tom and Rose had returned everything to its place and a few calls regarding potential clients had come in. There had been a short piece in the Niagara Gazette about Anton Proctor having to resign from his position as Director of Security at the casino and being replaced by Clarence Jimerson on an interim basis. Donovan hoped Jimerson got the gig on a full-time basis eventually. He was obviously suited for the job.

Shortly after 9 AM he entered his office from the back door. His mother heard him and came in from the reception area carrying a FedEx box and an open envelope on top of it.

"What's this?" Donovan asked.

"The box? I don't know," Rose replied. "The letter was hand delivered by your friend, Ms. Sherman from the State Department of Taxation and Finance with the files that I gave her." She set the box down on his desk.

Donovan picked up the envelope and took out the letter, the essence of which confirmed that the audit was over.

"Did she say anything?" he asked.

"Oh, she seemed quite put out. She said something about you doing contract word for the Federal Government and the state was told to stand down for the time being and how it all sounded pretty fishy."

"I am nothing if not a patriot," he said smiling. He looked up at Rose and she was not smiling back. She turned and went back to the reception area.

Watson had frowned when Donovan explained his problem with the State. He thought that maybe he had overstepped Watson's sense of gratitude. It was only after he swore he would carry Watson's secrets to the grave that Watson shook his head and said, "I can make a call," and kicked Donovan out of the Federal Building.

Donovan took a pocket knife out of his desk drawer and cut the tape on the box. Inside the box, wrapped in bubble wrap, was his laptop. He pulled it out and saw a folded piece of paper underneath it. He placed the laptop on the desk, removed the paper and unfolded it. There was a short handwritten note: *Friends don't shoot friends.* was all it said. The writing was almost childlike, as if it had been done with the non-dominant hand. Katrina had no doubt saved his life again the other night. And probably even spared it when she could just as easily have shot him in self-defense. She truly was an enigma.

A while later he heard the exterior door open to the reception area. "Hi, Mrs. Donovan," a woman's voice said.

"Carolyn! How nice to see you," Rose replied. "It's just Rose by the way and you look fantastic."

Donovan entered the reception area as Carolyn was saying, "Brandon wanted to try out for the Cross Country team at school and he made me run with him until I couldn't keep up any more." She noticed Donovan and smiled. Rose looked at Donovan and despite her mood smirked at him.

"We're going to Kosta's for a late breakfast," he said.

"Would you like to come with us," Carolyn offered.

"No," Rose said insistently. "You two go enjoy yourselves. Someone has to stay and direct this enterprise." She turned back to Donovan and he could have sworn she winked at him.

Donovan pulled on his jacket and held the door open for Carolyn. "Can we take your car?" he asked. "Mine is still at the shop."

"Sure, I'm just down the street."

Outside they turned right and Donovan saw Travis Parker getting out of the passenger side of a black BMW. The driver was the man with the glasses who had driven him back from the meeting the other day.

"Carolyn, you go ahead," Donovan said. "I'll be right there. She looked at him quizzically and then went off towards her car.

"Travis," Donovan said. He wasn't armed but hoped that Travis wasn't going to do anything rash in broad daylight.

"Tom," Parker nodded. His eyes went from watching Carolyn walk away back to Donovan. "I thought we should clear the air."

"I am all for doing that," Donovan replied.

"On one hand, I should be pretty pissed at you for getting up in my shit."

"And on the other hand?"

Parker smiled slightly. "On the other hand, you may have done me a favor. Anton Proctor was a piece of shit. I never trust a man who turns his back on his own people. And as far as Tiny goes, that's a mixed bag. You see the man in the Beemer?" Donovan glanced at the driver who was staring daggers at him. "Tiny was his half-brother and their mom is pretty upset. Still if your girl hadn't done what she did, we would not have known about our other problem."

"The undercover cop in your organization."

"Precisely," Parker nodded. "Right now, the only thing keeping my man there from getting even with you is the fact that he's the one who sponsored Devon Dixon in the first place." Parker looked back at the driver. "His brother is his punishment." Donovan bit his tongue when he felt like saying that Karma had caught up with Tiny Cantrell.

"So, you and me, we're good?" Donovan asked.

"We're good Tom. But if you and I ever meet as adversaries again, I might not be able to hold him off." He looked at Donovan full on again.

"I understand."

Parker added, "Oh, and I didn't send those men after your family. That's not what I do. They were looking for you." Parker turned and went back to the Beemer.

Donovan went past them with one more glance at the driver.

He was looking straight ahead as Parker was saying something to him. The Beemer pulled away from the curb and Donovan walked down to where Carolyn was parked.

"Who was that?" Carolyn asked as he pulled his seatbelt on.

"Just a guy I used to work with."

"Is everything OK? He looked pretty serious."

Donovan nodded. "Yeah, everything's fine. Man, am I hungry." Maybe he was lying about everything being fine, but it didn't feel like it. He felt like Travis Parker would be good to his word either way. He glanced at Carolyn, she had been through a lot herself, raising a son with Asperger's Syndrome more or less by herself and her brother being killed. Did he really want to mix her up in his messed up world? She looked at him and smiled. He needed something normal in his life, something good.

Epilogue

Two weeks later, Utica New York

The wind was blowing the light cloud cover across the sky and the leaves across the cemetery. The woman gingerly climbed out of the rental car, her arm in a sling. Holy Trinity Cemetery was large, so she had stopped at the administration office to ask where she could find the plot. It wasn't hard once she knew which section to look in. One freshly filled grave and one that looked like it had been there awhile, side by side with simple brass plaques on small iron stands:

Irene L Jaworski 1953-2017

Allison K Baker 1996-2015

The woman laid the small bouquet of flowers on Allison's grave and stepped back. She wondered if anyone cared enough or had the resources to buy proper headstones for Irene and her granddaughter. She thought about inquiring at the office on her way out.

The woman wasn't religious, or even spiritual for that matter. She had witnessed a lot of death in her time. Most didn't phase her, but a few did. Still she felt compelled to offer something. "You deserved better, sister," she said. With her good arm she pulled her coat tighter and turned to leave.

About the Author

David Coleman is a native of Buffalo, new York. He curently lives in Hamburg, New York with his wife and two daughters. For more information on David's writing please visit rustbeltwriter. com.

Acknowledgments

To my home based "focus group;" my wife Jeanne and daughters Emily and Liz. Also my friend and editor Cynthia Lehman for her efforts, constructive criticism and support. To my parents who taught me the value of books. And to all the people who read and gave such positive feedback on the Donovan series.

Made in United States
North Haven, CT
03 December 2021

11946792R00124